Duffy

Duffy

Dan Kavanagh

PANTHEON BOOKS

NEW YORK

To Pat Kavanagh

1

The day they cut Mrs McKechnie, not much else happened in West Byfleet. Not much happened in Pyrford either, or even in the whole of Guildford. It took a week's hard work to fill the crime page of the *Guildford Advertiser*, and even then it was mainly soft-collar, middle-class stuff: company frauds, menopausal shoplifting, dog licence evasion; occasionally there was a disco scuffle, though most of the kids were too scared of forfeiting their Y.C. membership for that. So when they cut Mrs McKechnie, you'd expect the *Advertiser's* story on Page Seven to have led with this fact; but it didn't. It led with the other thing the men did, the afterthought, the nasty, sick thing which even Big Eddy, with his sense of humour, didn't really approve of. That tells you something about journalists.

When Rosie McKechnie opened the front door of 'The Pines' in the middle of an August afternoon, she thought it was the gasman. Anyone else would have thought the same. When you get to the front door, see a shortish figure through the stained-glass panelling, undo the catch, and immediately hear the word 'Gas', you naturally think it's the gasman. You don't think about how long it was since you last had your meter read.

The little man came through the door fast, with his head down, and butted Mrs McKechnie hard in the left breast. Then he pinioned her arms to her sides and simply stood there holding on to her. She felt a sharp, continuing pain in her breast; she looked wildly down at the top of the little man's head and saw that his hair was covered in gauze; she looked up towards the open door and was

7

nerving herself to scream when the second man arrived. He sidled in, closed the door gently behind him, put his finger to the flat, fleshy area which was all that the stocking mask showed of his lips, and went,

'Shhhh.'

She felt calmer when he did this; then, suddenly, she felt very frightened indeed. She opened her mouth to scream, and at once the second man was by her side, his hand clamped over her face.

'Now, no mouth, Rosie,' he whispered, 'no mouth. We don't want mouth. We don't need mouth. Understand?'

She understood. She had little choice. One man was cracking two armfuls of ribs; the other was nearly suffocating her. She swivelled her eyes downwards and could only see a stockinged head against her pearls (oh God, my jewels); sideways, and she could only see a powerful forearm and a blur of brown pullover. She was alone. Mrs Brenan, the char, had left at twelve after dropping her weekly bottle of scent; the only other living thing in the house apart from the three of them was Godfrey, the cat.

The tall one was speaking again, straight into her ear.

'Now listen, Rosie, an' I'll tell you what we're doing. Or rather, I'll tell you what we're not doing. We ain't gonna kill you. We ain't gonna prong you. We ain't gonna hurt you. We ain't gonna steal nothing – well, not unless we see something we *really* fancy. Understand?'

He loosened his grip on her face; she began to open her mouth, changed her mind, and simply nodded.

'Good, Rosie, and no mouth, like I said. Now, we've only come to do one thing, and when we've done, we'll go. A'right?'

She nodded again.

'But we don't want you interfering with us, so I'm afraid we're going to have to tie you up a bit. A'right?'

She nodded. Her jaw hurt from the tall man's hand. The

little one hadn't spoken at all, merely held on with a sort of silent frenzy which reminded her of her courting days.

'What I'm going to do first is let go of your mouth, take this fucking mask off, and tie it round your eyes so we won't have to bother about you identifying us. Now, you could scream' (he always seemed to be just ahead of her thoughts) 'but if you do, I'll make sure your dentist gets a good month's work, darling. So – no – fucking – mouth,' he repeated slowly.

Then he softly let go of her face, moved behind her, ripped the stocking off his head, and quickly bound it round her eyes.

'Well done, darling. Now, the little fellow's going to take off his mask now, and put it round your mouth, 'cos we may have to go round the house a bit, and we wouldn't want to have to run back and shut you up.'

She felt her arms being released, and then just stood there, blindfold, as the two men bound her mouth. The stocking pulled her lips back harshly at the corners, then pressed her tongue back and seemed to fill up her entire mouth. It tasted nasty. One of the men knotted it firmly at the base of her skull.

'Sorry about the Brylcreem, darling,' said the tall man. He seemed to be the only one who spoke. 'It was Brylcreem or dandruff. We should of offered you the choice. Not too tight, is it?'

It was; it hurt at the edges of her mouth; it felt as if her lips were being split open. She nodded her head up and down.

'Oh, a bit tight, is it? Sorry about that, Rosie, but you must appreciate our problem. It just wouldn't do its job if it was any looser. Tell you what, this'll make you feel better. Other blokes who are in our line of work, what they do is, they fill your mouth up with cotton wool first. Not nice. Tickles the back of your froat. Makes some of

9

them frow up their stomachs. Heard of one case, some old geezer frowed up his stomach and choked to death on it. Nasty. Not nice, was it?'

He was clearly addressing the little man, who gave a grunt. Then she heard a soft tapping noise. From the tall man's reply, she worked out that the little one must have been tapping the face of his watch.

'O.K., mustn't let the grass grow under our feet. Hang about a sec, Rosie, don't go away.'

They left her for a couple of minutes, then came back and propelled her into what she worked out was her lounge. They sat her down in a wheel-backed dining chair which one of them must have brought from the kitchen. Then she felt her ankles being tied together with something that wasn't rope. Finally, they bound her hands.

'Now, that's two pairs of best nylons, Rosie. Best Marks and Sparks. Autumn Beige we picked for you. Thought that was the sort of shade someone like you might wear.' It wasn't, but why this familiarity anyway? If they'd come to steal something why didn't they just get on with it? But they couldn't just have come to steal, else why would they have bothered to find out her name? How did they manage to come on one of the two afternoons when she didn't regularly have friends round, or go out to bridge? Had they been watching the house? They must have been. And what the hell did they want? How long would it be before Brian came home? Maybe they were after Brian for some reason? No, they couldn't be – they wouldn't have come so early if they'd wanted Brian.

The tall man with the quiet voice with bits of London rough in it was still going on about the stockings.

'Two pairs of frees, Rosie. Better than having the Fuller's brush man round, isn't it? I mean, if you don't like the shade, you can always give them away, can't you? I should look on the nylons as the silver lining to this little business, Rosie, I really would. An' as I say, if they don't

10

fit you, they might fit Barbara, mightn't they? Yes, I think they might fit Barbara.'

Rosie McKechnie didn't know anyone called Barbara. She might have known a Barbara or two in her teens or twenties, but she didn't know anyone called Barbara now. She was in her late forties, and couldn't remember meeting a Barbara for twenty years. So why had the man repeated the name? It sounded so deliberate.

There was a pause. When the tall man started speaking again, his tone was almost apologetic.

'I'm afraid we come to the hard bit now, Rosie. You see, we had to tell you a little lie to begin with, just to get you to co-operate. Well, two lies, actually, I suppose. I mean, we aren't from the gas, either.'

He paused again. Rosie was suddenly very frightened indeed. Her body told her she was frightened. She felt a trickle of pee come from her, then stop.

'It's a'right, we ain't gonna kill you, we don't deal in that. We ain't gonna prong you, neither, though, if you'll allow me to say so, Mr McKechnie's a very lucky man. But I'm afraid we're gonna have to cut you just a little. It'll hurt a bit – there's no way we can avoid that, but we'll try and make it hurt as little as possible. I mean, we're not sadists, you know. And the boss did make his instructions very clear. So it won't be as bad as it could be.'

Rosie McKechnie began to cry into her blindfold. She was sure they were going to cut her face. The face that Brian had picked out from the chorus line of *Ahoy There!* on a foggy evening in November 1952. He'd picked it out from the sixth row of the stalls, despite the fact that she was wearing a matelot suit and had a silly cap on her head with a red bobble on the top of it. In France, Brian had explained to her, girls go up to sailors and ask if they can touch their bobbles for luck; the price is a kiss. When Brian had arrived backstage with a bunch of Michaelmas daisies and asked if he could touch her bobble, she hadn't

11

understood; or rather, she thought she'd understood all too clearly. But he hadn't meant that, as he'd explained to her over dinner. And that was when he first called her 'My little chorus girl'. Now his little chorus girl, the one he'd picked out from the sixth row, was going to have her face cut. She knew it.

'Time for Stanley, I'm afraid,' said the tall man softly. Stanley: that must be the little fellow's name; she'd better remember it. 'Now, Mrs McKechnie,' (he had suddenly become formal) 'what we're going to do is make a little cut, just a nick really, round about your shoulder.' Thank God – they weren't going for her face. 'Now it'll hurt a bit, but you ain't going to bleed too hard, few stitches, eight to ten I'd say, and, well, no backless dresses for a while, but you'll be surprised how quickly you'll get over it.'

She waited. There was nothing else she could do but wait and see what happened next.

What happened next was that the little man dug in his pocket and pulled out a thick, heavy lino-cutting knife with a retractable blade. It was gunmetal blue, and had a little serrated catch on the top which, when you slid it forward, brought the blade into view. At a sign from the tall man, he walked out of the lounge, down a corridor past a few framed theatre bills, and into the kitchen. He didn't notice Godfrey sitting on the dresser; but Godfrey certainly noticed him.

Godfrey was the McKechnies' large, paunchy, grey-haired tom cat. A big, swaggery, macho cat with firm ideas about territoriality. The sort of cat who would pin females up against the wall and accuse them of being frigid if they wouldn't submit. Even in the feline world, where selfishness and cunning are cardinal virtues, Godfrey was an outstandingly mean cat. Other cats fought shy of him; some of the smaller local dogs had been seen crossing the road to avoid him; not even his owners really liked him.

12

They gave him everything he needed and stayed out of his way as much as possible.

As the little man passed the dresser, he heard a sharp, sibilant hiss. He turned and saw Godfrey. The little man thought he knew his way round cats, and he reached out a hand to tickle Godfrey's chin. Godfrey didn't like his chin being tickled; he didn't really like humans coming near him. As the hand approached, he slashed at it with his right paw.

Godfrey kept his claws in good trim. Three white lines appeared on the back of the man's hand; after a few seconds they seemed to pop, and beads of blood appeared. The man looked at his hand disbelievingly. He stood there and glanced slowly round the kitchen. When his eye fell on the fridge-freezer, he suddenly shot out a hand and grabbed Godfrey by the neck before he could move, walked quickly across the kitchen, pulled open the door of the freezer section, threw the cat in, and slammed the door. He turned, and looked round the kitchen again: bar area, concealed ceiling lighting, stainless steel surfaces, gadgets everywhere; a cooker with an eye-level spit-roaster. He nodded to himself.

Then he walked over to the sink and ran the cold tap. First he washed the blood off his hand, and held it there for a couple of minutes to try and stop the bleeding. After that he filled a kettle and set it to boil. When the steam began to rise from the spout, he took his blue knife, unsheathed the blade, and held it in the steam for about a minute.

When he got back to the lounge the tall man was looking impatient for the first time that afternoon. The back of the woman's dress was now open.

'Took yer time.'

The little man held out his right hand and spoke the only two words Rosie McKechnie ever heard him say.

'Focking caht.' It was a lighter voice than the other

man's with a strong flavour of Irish in it. A few fresh beads of blood were beginning to pop on his hand as he took the knife in his right hand, laid his left flat on the middle of the woman's back, bent her forwards, and made a sudden but careful vertical incision in her right shoulder a couple of inches away from the strap of her bra. The pressure on the knife made the blood run again from the little man's hand; automatically, he brushed it off on the back of the woman's dress.

The tall man was speaking again.

'Three inches. The boss said three inches.' Rosie was bent right forward now, hunched with pain. 'And three inches it seems to be.' He crouched down beside the gagged woman and spoke to her almost gently. 'Lean back, love, you're only making yourself bleed more like that.' She sat up, trying not to pull on the wound. 'Eight to ten, you'll need, I reckon. Maybe twelve. You'll be O.K. We could give you some drink if you like.'

She shook her head. She didn't drink spirits; never had. A glass of brandy now was more likely to make her throw up than the taste of hair cream from the little man's mask.

'We'll be off soon,' said the tall man.

The little man took the knife back to the kitchen to wash it off. He turned on the cold tap, held the blade under it for a minute or so, dried it on a J-cloth, and returned the knife to his pocket. Then he put his hand under the tap again, though the blood by now had almost stopped coming. With his handkerchief he dabbed dry the three parallel red weals on the back of his hand, and walked across to the cooker with the eye-level spit-roaster. He turned one of the switches to Full, and then wandered thoughtfully across towards the fridge-freezer.

Back in the lounge, the tall man was loosening the stocking over Mrs McKechnie's eyes.

'Now, if you shake your head a lot, this should work itself off in a bit,' he said. 'Sorry we can't do more for you, but you must understand our position. We gotta do what the boss says. It isn't worth anyone's while not doing what the boss says.'

She heard the sound of the little man returning from the kitchen.

'All cleared up in there?' the tall man asked, and got a grunt in reply. 'Yeah, I've wiped here as well,' he went on, and then turned towards Rosie McKechnie for the last time.

'Well, so long, Rosie, we'll be off now. Oh, and, er, hope the stockings fit. Fit someone, anyway.'

A few seconds later the front door closed quietly. Mrs McKechnie felt her dress wet to the waist with her own blood. She scarcely had the strength to shake the gag free from her eyes. Eventually it fell off, and she found herself staring out of the window at her back garden. At least, she thought, they haven't cut my face. At least they haven't taken anything. At least they haven't smashed things out of malice, like burglars are supposed to do. But then, were they burglars anyway? Brian would be home in a few hours; he would be able to tell her what had happened; to tell her why.

When Brian got back from London he thought his wife had burnt the dinner again. A heavy, slow, red-faced man, he stood in the hall puffing from his walk from the station, uncertain whether to go into the kitchen or the lounge first. From the kitchen came a pungent smell of burning, though somehow it wasn't the charred-dinner smell he'd had to get used to over the years; it was something odder, sharper. It smelt as if mattresses were being singed. From the lounge he could hear muffled sobs: Rosie blubbing again about having spoiled his dinner. Her tears always disarmed whatever irritation he felt on these occasions.

Brian was a considerate husband, and he headed for the lounge rather than the kitchen. A few more minutes'

charring wouldn't make much difference. Then he saw
Rosie tied to the chair. He rushed across to her and was
about to put his heavy arms around her when he saw the
blood. He untied her mouth gag, then freed her wrists
and feet. As he held her head between his palms and
kissed her on the cheeks and forehead, she looked at him
with the eyes of a lost child and couldn't manage a word.
After a minute or so of this traumatised silence he went to
the phone and called his private doctor; then he called the
police. As he put the phone down and walked back
towards her, Rosie suddenly spoke.

'Who's Barbara?'

'Barbara? I don't know. Why?'

But she merely replied, 'Who's Barbara?' in a distant
voice.

McKechnie frowned and hurried off to try and rescue
what was left of the dinner. Barbara was the name of his
current mistress. But she was a mistress of only a few
weeks – how could anyone have found out? And why
bother? What had it got to do with his wife being
assaulted? Why were the Georgian candlesticks still safely
on the lounge table? Why had nothing been touched?

When he reached the kitchen, he discovered there was
something in the house which had been touched. What
was revolving slowly on the eye-level spit-roaster was
definitely not Brian McKechnie's dinner.

2

The doctor came, inserted thirteen stitches, sedated Mrs McKechnie, and put her to bed. An hour later two policemen arrived, apologising for the delay and blaming it on undermanning; they discovered that the victim was heavily drugged, asked Mr McKechnie a few questions without getting anywhere, told him not to touch anything – 'What do you mean, *anything*?' he replied – took a cursory look at doors and windows, and said they would be back the next day.

Mr McKechnie sat over a bowl of Heinz oxtail soup wondering why anyone should want to attack his wife and tell her the name of his mistress at the same time. He wasn't aware of having any particular enemies. His mistress, who doubled as his secretary, wasn't married; and though she wore her hair prettily coiled up on the top of her head, smiled at strangers and waggled her bottom more than she needed to when she walked, he wasn't aware of having any rivals for her affections. Besides, if a rival did come along, Brian wasn't that attached to her: if she wanted to go, she could. His days of fighting to keep a woman were over. Not, for that matter, that he was in any state to fight. The only exercise he ever took was with a knife and fork; he panted after climbing stairs, sweated a great deal, was moderately overweight, and only the previous year had had a minor, admonitory heart attack.

The next day a detective-sergeant from the Guildford C.I.D. sat on Rosie McKechnie's bed with a colleague. Gradually they pieced together what she knew; though mostly it was what she didn't know. A tall man with a roughish Cockney accent and a brown pullover; a short

17

man with a possibly Irish accent who had 'passed a re-mark', as Rosie delicately put it, about Godfrey. The short man might have been called Stanley. There had been two – almost three – deliberate mentions of someone called Barbara. There had been mentions of someone called the Boss.

'Had any quarrels, Mrs McKechnie?'

'No – I don't quarrel. Except with the char. What sort of quarrels?'

'Oh, arguments, disagreements, you know, *words*, that sort of thing.'

'No.'

'Know anyone called Stanley?'

'Well, there's Brian's uncle, but . . .'

'We understand, madam. What about Barbara?'

'I've been trying to think. No, no one, absolutely no one.'

'Well, looks like we'll have to rely on forensics. Unless your husband can give us any assistance, of course.'

The two policemen walked slowly downstairs with Mr McKechnie.

'Problems, sir,' said Bayliss, the detective-sergeant, a sandy-haired, slightly truculent man in a blue suit. 'Problems. No identification; or none that doesn't leave us with most of the population of England under suspicion. No dabs, according to my colleague. No theft. No obvious motive, you'll agree?'

'None that I can see.'

'And a particularly vicious crime. Not forgetting the cat, of course. Now the problem is, work of a maniac, pair of maniacs, or not? If it were just the cat, I'd say yes. There are some pretty sick people about. I've known maniacs toss cats off high buildings, just for kicks. But spitting and roasting, that's something new to me. What about you, Willett?'

His colleague thought for a bit about the crimes against

18

felines that he'd come across. 'I've had drownings, and I've had, you know, mutilations,' he replied. 'I've heard about a jerry-can job, but that was some time ago. Nothing like this.'

'But then you see, sir,' went on Bayliss, 'the injury to your wife seemed planned, didn't it? I mean, they knew her name, they seemed to know when she'd be in, and, if you'll excuse me, they knew exactly what they intended to do to her. Didn't they?'

'You're the experts.'

'Yes, I suppose we are. Kind of you to say so, sir. So what I'm driving at, sir, is motive. Now, Willett, what did Mrs McKechnie say they said about this Stanley fellow?'

Willett opened his notebook and turned back a few pages. 'Something like, "Time for Stanley", she said she thought the tall one said.'

'"Time for Stanley". Almost sounds as if he was letting the other one loose. Sort of letting him off the leash, almost. Know any Stanleys, sir?'

'My uncle, but . . . '

'No, quite. No one else?'

'Afraid not.'

'All right. Now, let's turn to the easy one. Who's Barbara?'

'I've no idea.'

'You a bit of a ladies' man, are you, sir?'

'What do you mean? Certainly not.'

'Never played around at all, sir? You must have had your chances, if you don't mind the phrase. Never stepped out of line?'

'Certainly not. I'm fifty-five. I had a heart attack last year. I should think the exercise would kill me.' (It was true, Barbara and he did have to take it a bit easy every so often; it would be a great way to go, he used to think, if only he were able to face the embarrassment. Though of course, he probably wouldn't be there to face it.)

'So you and Mrs McKechnie . . . ?' Bayliss was doubtless referring to the fact that Rosie had her own bedroom.

'Since you seem to get a kick out of knowing that sort of thing, the answer's no, actually, we don't any more. We're still great friends, though.'

'I don't doubt it sir, not for a minute. Now what about your wife? Does she . . . have any callers?'

'What the hell makes you think you've got the right to ask that sort of question? My wife's been knifed, she hasn't been raped. Why don't you look for the weapon or something? What on earth is the point of this sort of questioning?'

'Well, you don't always know that till you get the answers. So, no Stanley, no Barbara; no fannying about; and what about this person called the Boss?'

'Could be anyone. Everyone's got a boss.'

'I suppose that's true, Mr McKechnie. It's a funny tale though, isn't it? I mean, here are these two people who break into your house, assault your wife, kill your cat, and mention three people's names, and nobody seems to know anything about any of them. Who's *your* boss, Mr McKechnie?' Bayliss didn't seem particularly friendly.

'I'm my own boss.'

'Tell us about what you're boss of, Mr McKechnie.'

McKechnie and Co Ltd. Registered company. Trading head office Rupert Street, W.1. Importers and distributors of toys, jokes, novelties, disguises, indoor fireworks, magic kits and funny masks. Policemen's helmets for sale, though strictly in junior sizes. Trade a bit seasonal, low in summer, high towards Christmas, naturally. No business difficulties. Turnover in six figures. Stock in trade held in two small warehouses, one in Lexington Street and one in a little courtyard off Greek Street. A small, profitable, honest business. That was McKechnie's story.

'Sounds almost too good to be true, sir. You wouldn't

mind if we came up one day and talked to you at your office?'

'Of course not. I'm going to stay at home and look after my wife for the rest of the week. You can come and see me, if there's any point in it, early next week.'

'That's very co-operative of you, sir. Now about this end of things. I'll be sending the police surgeon round tomorrow to have a look at your wife's wound – see if he's got any sort of an idea what the weapon was. We'll take away the cat, if that's all right with you; and we'd like the dress your wife was wearing too. And if you do remember about any of those names, you'll let us know, won't you, sir?'

'Of course.'

As soon as the police had left, McKechnie called his office. Barbara answered the phone; she was bound to – she was the only person there. He asked her if he hadn't always been nice to her, and she said he had. He asked her if she'd do him a favour and she said she hoped it was the same one as usual because she enjoyed it. He said no, not this time, you little temptress, it was a bit different. He'd had a few problems which he'd explain to her some other time. He wanted her to close down the office and take three weeks' paid holiday. No, she could still have her annual three weeks as well, at a later date. No, he wasn't trying to tell her she was being sacked. Yes, he was still very fond of her. Yes, they'd do that again soon too. Soon, soon. And he'd send a cheque for a month's salary to her home address.

He made a second phone call, to a temp agency in Shaftesbury Avenue, and asked for a secretary for a couple of weeks, starting the following Monday. Then he sat down and wondered whether he was doing the right thing.

This was on a Tuesday. On the Wednesday the police surgeon came, examined Mrs McKechnie, offered his condolences about Godfrey, and left, muttering about Islamic methods of punishment.

On the Thursday two things happened. The *Guildford Advertiser* came out, with a headline halfway down Page Seven reading: BIZARRE PET DEATH IN MYSTERY BREAK-IN: MANIACS HUNTED. And Det-Sgt Bayliss turned up again with Willett in tow.

'We've had the surgeon's report,' said Bayliss, 'and I think we can rule out your Uncle Stanley.' McKechnie looked puzzled. Bayliss pulled out a short, typed document from his briefcase and read from it: '"Victim . . . Wound . . . Surrounding Area . . ." Ah, here we are, "Possible Instrument: medium to heavy knife with fine blade. Small area of blade used, so probably not flick-knife type of instrument, or sharpened domestic knife. Some sort of modelling knife, perhaps, or specialist wood-cutting instrument. No evidence of previous usage of the instrument was obtainable, since the wound had already been thoroughly cleansed by time of police examination; but possibly some specialist instrument, like a Stanley knife."'

Bayliss looked up and smiled in a self-satisfied way; then he nodded to Willett, who dug in his notebook and quoted back Mrs McKechnie's words: '"Something like 'Time for Stanley'".'

Bayliss still looked pleased with himself. McKechnie couldn't imagine why the neutralisation of one of the very few clues Bayliss had should afford him any pleasure. Bayliss explained,

'Well, before we were looking for everyone called Stanley. Now we're only looking for people with Stanley knives. It must increase our chances a little.'

McKechnie didn't know if he was being flippant or simply foolish.

The following week Bayliss and Willett came up to McKechnie's Rupert Street office. They were shown in by his new secretary, Belinda. He'd deliberately told the agency that he wanted a really efficient girl because he was fed up with tarts in short skirts who doubled the size of his Tipp-Ex bill and tried to make up for it by flashing their panties at him when they were filing. The agency understood what he was saying, wrote 'Religious' on the back of his card in their private shorthand, and sent him Belinda, a girl with a slight limp who wore a huge silver cross between her breasts as if to ward off sweaty male hands. McKechnie was happy with her, even though she wasn't noticeably more efficient than the girls who cutely pointed their gussets at him on their first afternoon.

As Bayliss arrived, he asked casually how long Belinda had worked there; but McKechnie was already prepared for that. He always had temps, he said, because he found them more reliable, and it wasn't hard to master the work, and he sometimes closed down the office for a few weeks, and anyway, the office was too small to risk getting stuck with a secretary you didn't get along with. Oh, he got them from all sorts of temp agencies – sometimes one, sometimes another; he couldn't even remember where he'd got Belinda from – they could ask her if they wanted to. His previous secretary's name? Oh, Sheila, and before that, Tracy, and before that, oh, Millie or something.

When Bayliss and Willett left, McKechnie felt as if he had just pulled off a deal. He walked up to Bianchi's and treated himself to the best the kitchen could offer, just to show how pleased he was with himself.

The next week he got the first phone call. Belinda told him that there was a Mr Salvatore on the line.

'Mr McKechnie?

'Yes.'

'And how are you today?'

'Fine.'

'Quite sure you're all right?'

'Yes, quite. What can I do for you?' These immigrants

23

did go on a bit – thought it was all part of British civility. McKechnie knew one Greek retailer who, by the time he got to the end of all his preliminary bowing and scraping, had usually forgotten what he was ringing about. Then he had to ring back with his order later.

'And your wife, Mr McKechnie, is she well?'

McKechnie bridled, though the man's tone hadn't changed. 'She's fine. What can I do for you?'

'Because where I come from, we have a saying – a man's wife is the centrepiece of his table. Don't you think that is a pretty phrase, a gallant phrase?'

McKechnie hung up. Whoever the man was, he could either come to the point or bugger off. Besides, McKechnie wanted a little time to think what might be going on.

He didn't get it. The phone went again almost at once, and Belinda said apologetically,

'You're reconnected, Mr McKechnie. Sorry you got cut off, one of my fingers must have slipped.' That was the sort of secretary you got nowadays – the old sort, and even some of the gusset-flashers, at least knew when they'd cut you off. This lot didn't know whether they had or not; they merely assumed – and it was a correct assumption – that they had.

'Terrible, this telephone system of yours, Mr McKechnie,' said the voice. 'They tell me it all went wrong with nationalisation, but of course I do not remember that myself.'

'Are you calling me on business, Mr . . .'

'Salvatore. Well, yes and no, as you say. I am not in the business of ringing up strangers simply to reduce the Post Office's deficit, anyway. So, I tell you why I am ringing. I am ringing to say that I am sorry about the cat.'

'The . . .'

'Yes, Mr McKechnie, it was, how shall I say, you understand French, Mr McKechnie, it showed *un peu trop d'enthousiasme.* In simple language, the lads got carried away.'

'You . . . fucker.' McKechnie didn't really know what to say; he didn't in fact care much about the cat; it had always been, as she herself put it, Rosie's baby.

'Well, I accept your rebuke. Now, the second thing I have to say is, I hope very much that your lady wife is recovering from her unpleasant ordeal. And I suggest that you do not hang up.' The tone had hardened. McKechnie did not reply. The voice went on. 'Well, I take the liberty of inferring from your silence that she is, as you put it, on the mend.'

Again, McKechnie did not reply.

'And the third thing I have to say to you is this. Don't you think it is extraordinary that the police have no idea what might have happened, or why, or who would have done such a thing? By the way, I assume you did not tell them about your pretty secretary who seems not to be working for you any more?'

McKechnie still did not reply. He was trying to write down on his telephone pad as much as possible of the conversation.

'No, you did not. I think I can tell that. So, if I may sum up, Mr McKechnie, what I am saying to you is this. Isn't it extraordinary, and isn't it a little frightening, that two such unpleasant things could happen in your very own home, and that the police, after full investigation, have found no clues that are of any use to them? Is it not ironic that the one clue which might have been of use was denied to them by you? It is not a pretty situation, is it, Mr McKechnie, at least not for you? I mean, the point is, isn't it, that something similar, or even, though I do hesitate to say so, something quite a lot worse, could happen, and you would be fairly certain that once again the police would not be able to be of any assistance? What do you say to that, Mr McKechnie?'

'I say, you never can tell.'

'And I say to you, Mr McKechnie, that some of us can, some of us can tell. I mean, take the present case. Say you go back to your police. Say you tell them you're sorry, you lied, you didn't tell them about Barbara. Do you think that would make them redouble their energies, if you went and told them you had been lying to them? They are only human, after all, Mr McKechnie, they would merely think you had been telling more lies, they would probably say to each other, as you put it, "Stuff him". And then, if they did take you seriously, where has this new piece of information taken them? How much nearer are they to their quarry? There are other crimes every day, even in your neck of the woods.'

'What do you want?'

'Ah, I am happy that you asked me that, Mr McKechnie. It shows at least that you are not a stupid man. What I want you to do is to *think*. What I want you to think about is what people call the angles. That is all that I want you to do, for the moment. And now I will get off this line and let you go about your lawful business.'

The phone was put down.

McKechnie dutifully started to think about the angles. Was he being preshed? Not yet, anyway. Was he being softened up for being preshed? If so, they were going about it in a pretty extreme manner. Was his wife safe at home? Was he safe? Should he go back to the Guildford police? Should he go along to the station here, West Central, up in Broadwick Street? Should he perhaps try and get the investigation transferred to West Central, and hope that the bit about Barbara would get dropped on the way? But what did he really have to tell them here? One thing he could do was go and have a chat to Shaw, the detective-sergeant at West Central he'd had a few drinks with now and then. Maybe he'd do that.

He rang West Central, and was told that Shaw was on

holiday for a week. Did he want to talk to anyone else? No, he didn't.

Two days later Belinda buzzed him and said she had Mr Salvatore on the line again.

'Mr McKechnie, still well? Good. I won't take up all that much of your time. I take it you've had your think. You haven't been back and made your little confession, of course.'

McKechnie was silent.

'No, of course you haven't. Now, I'll tell you what you're going to do for me. You're going to give me some money. Not very much money. Very little money, really. Twenty pounds. No, let's say twenty-five. Now, you go to your bank in the morning – or you take it from your float, I really don't mind which – and you wait for me to ring again and tell you what I want you to do with it. It's quite straightforward, Mr McKechnie. Oh, and you can be assured that even if you haven't done this before, I have.'

The phone went dead. McKechnie took a deep breath, put on his jacket, told Belinda he was going out for a few minutes, and walked round to West Central police station.

West Central was one of those stations which they kept on not getting around to modernising. Ten years ago they took away the blue lamp mounted on its wall bracket, and five years after that they put up a new sign, a long thin white one, lit by a neon tube, which said WEST CENTRAL POLICE STATION. But then things slowed down considerably: the grey paint inside got blacker; the canteen plates got more chipped by the year; tempers got shorter.

Shaw was still on holiday, and instead McKechnie was shown in to see Superintendent Ernest Sullivan, twenty-five years in the force, ten on this patch, a surly, fleshy man unimpressed by all forms of crime and by most forms of complainant. McKechnie told his story – the assault on his wife, the spitting of his cat, the phone calls, the

27

demand for money – while Sullivan shuffled some papers round his desk and occasionally picked his ears with a matchstick.

When he'd finished, Sullivan merely said,

'Never heard the cat thing before. Heard the rest before. Must take quite a bit of strength to push a spit through a cat. Probably get scratched, wouldn't you?'

McKechnie was impatient with the amount of interest shown by the police in the death of his cat.

'What about the wounding of my wife and the blackmail?'

'How do you know it is blackmail?'

'Well of course it's blackmail.'

'Did the man say what he'd do if you didn't pay?'

'No.'

'Then maybe he's just trying it on. Maybe the two things aren't connected. Maybe he just read your local paper and thought he'd try his luck.'

That couldn't be the case, McKechnie thought, as the Salvatore fellow had known about Barbara, and nothing of that had been in the paper. But all he said was, 'Not very likely, is it?'

'It's possible.' Sullivan seemed keen for the case to give him the minimum trouble. McKechnie waited. Eventually, Sullivan shifted in his seat, picked his ear again, and said, 'I suppose I could get the case transferred up here.' He showed little sign of enthusiasm. 'Shall I do that?'

'If you think that's best. Whatever's happening, it's obviously got nothing to do with where I live.'

Sullivan nodded, got slowly to his feet, and disappeared. When he came back, he seemed, if possible, even less keen on McKechnie's presence in his office. If only McKechnie would go away, his look implied, he could get on and give his ears a real cleaning out.

'Well, they're sending me the file,' he said. 'Chap named Bayliss. Said that forensics reported the cat had

28

been on the spit for about three hours. Nasty smell, was there?'

'I don't remember.'

'Come, come, Mr McKechnie, I'm sure you do. And, er, while we're on the subject of nasty smells, there's a bit of a one in here, isn't there?'

McKechnie looked round.

'No, you don't need to look round. I mean, there's a bit of a nasty smell coming from your chair, isn't there, Mr McKechnie? Not always kept our own nose exactly clean, have we? Bit of a fiddler, really, aren't you, Mr McKechnie? It is going to be McKechnie for a bit longer, isn't it? Because if you're thinking of changing again, I'd better nip out and update our file.'

'That was all years ago.'

It had also been two hundred miles away. A bit of bad company, temptation, it could happen to anybody. You can't run a business without being tempted occasionally. But how had Sullivan got hold of his record?

'It's all years ago,' he repeated. 'I thought there was a Rehabilitation of Offenders Act or something.'

'There is, Mr McKechnie, there is.' Sullivan was livening up. He seemed to be enjoying this part of the conversation. 'But it doesn't apply to us, now, does it? Or not the way they meant it to. And when someone moves into our patch, in however small a way, we like to know just a little about him.'

'Well, you know, Superintendent, you can't run a business without being tempted occasionally.'

'Yes, I'm sure, Mr McKechnie. I'm just surprised, reading our little file on you, that there weren't more road accidents up in Leeds.' He chuckled. 'What with all this stuff falling off the backs of lorries.'

McKechnie was silent.

'Still, I suppose we'd better let bygones be bygones.' Sullivan sounded as if he didn't hope to convince even himself of this principle, let alone anyone else.

'Turning to my current problem, Superintendent.'

'Of course, of course.'

'What should I do about the twenty-five quid?'

'Pay it and write it off against tax as a bad debt.'

'Are you serious?'

'Completely. Isn't that what your natural instinct would be to do? Isn't that what any self-respecting fiddler would do?'

'You're telling me to piss off, aren't you?'

'No, I'm not, I'm merely saying Business is business. Your business involves writing off small amounts of money every so often. My business involves not wasting the time of my men if some local villain reads a Guildford newspaper and squeezes a pony out of another local fiddler. Funny how private enterprise springs up, isn't it, Mr McKechnie? We had a villain once, he used to read the deaths column in the *Telegraph*, and send out small bills for tailoring alterations addressed to the dead man. The deceased's family used to get the bill – it was only four or five quid, he wasn't greedy – and most of the time they paid up. Natural instinct, really. Mean not to pay your dearly beloved's bills, isn't it?'

'What went wrong?'

'Ah, yes, something always goes wrong, doesn't it? Except that sometimes nothing goes wrong, and then there's no story at all. What went wrong was as simple as what went right: he made the mistake of sending in a bill to a deceased member of a family tailoring business. Everyone was quite amused really. No one was hurt, I suppose. He only did a couple of years.'

'Have you heard of this man called Salvatore?'

'Oh yes, I've heard of Salvatore. Big local villain. Girls, smokes, bit of smack, mossing, tweedling; a very democratic villain, Mr Salvatore.'

McKechnie was surprised; and cross. 'Why didn't you

tell me earlier? Now you can tap his phone when he calls me tomorrow.'

'Patience, Mr McKechnie.' Sullivan seemed to be enjoying himself again; he'd even forgotten about his ears. 'We can't tap phones like that, you know. All sorts of red tape involved. Have to get Home Office permission; Home Secretary's signature. Now he wouldn't give his signature for a pony's worth of squeeze, would he?'

'Why not?'

'Well, I'll tell you why not, Mr McKechnie. Because Mr Salvatore no speaka da English, only speaka da Eyetalian. Tutto his life. And in the second place, he isn't with us any more. He died about five years ago. Nice old fellow. All the boys here chipped in for a wreath.'

'So who did I talk to?'

'Well, there aren't any other Salvatores around. So I reckon you've got yourself a joker, Mr McKechnie, that's what I reckon you've got.'

'So what do I do?'

'You do what you like, Mr McKechnie. You pay up if you want to, you tell him to fuck off if you want to.'

'And if he doesn't fuck off?'

'Well, put it this way. If he carries on and gets up to a ton, you come back and see me. Under a ton, it's just not worth our while.' There was a meaningful look in Sullivan's eye as he said this. Was he giving McKechnie a price?

The next morning, Brian took Rosie breakfast in bed, as he had done every morning since the attack, and sat downstairs with his paper and the letters. They had always opened each other's letters; it seemed a sign of how close they were. There were a couple of business letters for Brian, some circulars, and a small brown envelope addressed to Mrs B. McKechnie. It felt fatter in one corner than elsewhere, and the envelope seemed a little stained. He opened it carefully, looked inside, and

31

then glanced quickly towards the stairs in case Rosie might be coming down.

The first thing he withdrew from the envelope was a photo of Barbara. It wasn't one he'd seen before. She was walking down a street, somewhere in London by the looks of it; to judge from the angle of the photograph, it might have been taken from a passing car. It was a good likeness, but he couldn't tell quite how pretty she was looking because the photograph was stained. Half her face had been smudged where the emulsion had run. He looked in the envelope again and saw why: a used condom was slowly leaking its contents. He screwed the envelope up and pushed it into his pocket. Then he turned over the photograph. Typed on the back, in capitals, he read:

DEAR MRS MCKECHNIE WE THOUGHT YOU MIGHT LIKE TO
SEE A SNAP OF BARBARA

McKechnie looked back at the photo. He gradually made out one or two of the out-of-focus street signs – a clothes shop, a bank, a theatre. It had been taken in Shaftesbury Avenue, just round the corner from his office.

On his way to work he threw away the envelope with the condom in it. At his desk, he tried to think about that morning's orders, but instead found himself waiting all the time for the phone to go. Eventually, of course, it did.

'Mr McKechnie, and how are you today? As well as always, I trust?'

'Fine.'

'Your wife well?'

'Yes, why shouldn't she be?'

'Why indeed. Unless, of course, she didn't enjoy opening her letters this morning.'

'I wouldn't know – I left before the post came.' He wasn't quite sure why he lied; he was just fed up with being outguessed all the time.

'Anyway, to business. We're a little displeased with

you, Mr McKechnie. You'll understand why, of course.'

'No.'

'Come, come, it really was very silly of you to go to the police. What makes you think that one branch of the police force is likely to be any more efficient than another? I'm sure they can't have been much help to you.' (He didn't know how right he was) 'Anyway, since you seem interested in raising the risk, I'm afraid I'm going to have to raise the stakes. The twenty-five goes up to fifty because of your little indiscretion. But, just to show you that you're dealing with businessmen, you can have another day to pay. Fifty by tomorrow, and I'll ring you in the morning about delivery.'

'How do I know you're serious?'

'Suck it and see, Mr McKechnie, suck it and see.' The phone went dead.

He rang Sullivan and explained what had happened; Sullivan didn't seem at all pleased to be hearing from him so soon. He grunted once, said 'Pay it', and put the phone down.

After a night's reflection, McKechnie went to the bank early the next day and withdrew fifty pounds. It was just possible that Sullivan was right; that it was a one-off job. But the more he thought about it, the less likely it seemed. He had a very unpleasant feeling that this was the start of something which could go on a long time. But he thought he'd take it gently to start with. At eleven o'clock the phone went again. This time the voice was brusquer.

'Brown envelope, please, Mr McKechnie. Two rubber bands round it, one in each direction. If by any foolish plan you asked the bank for new notes, go back and change them. Drop the envelope in the middle dustbin by the back entrance to the Columbia cinema at one o'clock.

McKechnie did exactly as he was told. He got to the middle dustbin on time, lifted the lid, dropped the envelope into the half-filled bin, turned, squinted round a bit to see if he could catch anyone spying on him, then marched off purposefully. He walked west along Shaftesbury Avenue, turned down the lower stub of Wardour Street, doubled back along Gerrard Street and stopped by an advertising hoarding. From here he could just make out, when traffic and pedestrians allowed, the three dustbins by the back entrance to the cinema. He'd been there twenty minutes or so, worrying each time a bus blocked his line of sight, when he gradually became conscious of a man watching him from a distance of about ten feet. A broad-faced, gingery, fleshy man with glasses and a slightly wild look in his eye. When he saw that McKechnie's attention was on him, he walked slowly towards him, then round behind him, then laid his chubby chin on McKechnie's shoulder so that they were now both looking across towards the dustbins, then turned sideways and grinned straight into McKechnie's face, then came round the front again, then took a big freckled thumb and forefinger and playfully grabbed a stretch of McKechnie's cheek, then said, with a friendly, slightly mad smile,

'Scram.'

McKechnie scrammed back to his office, his heart beating too fast for its own good.

Two weeks later 'Salvatore' called again.

'My dear Mr McKechnie, how nice to be talking to you again. It was so kind of you to help me out the other week when I was short. I'm sure the Revenue will understand when you put it through your books. Now, I do seem to be having a bit of a cash-flow problem again. I wonder if you could possibly help me out. I'm afraid I need just a little more this time, though. I think we'd better settle for a hundred.'

'I don't do that sort of business.'

'Well, Mr McKechnie, I don't happen to believe you. I'm sure a man with two warehouses and an office, however meagre they are, can find a hundred pounds to help out a friend.' McKechnie paused. He was wondering why Salvatore, who had had a fairly strong foreign accent during his first call, now seemed to be speaking almost standard English. He answered,

'All right.'

Secretly McKechnie was pleased. Now the police would have to act. He rang Sullivan and told him the demand had gone up to the level which justified his interest. The next day he did as instructed, made the drop at one o'clock in a litter bin strapped to a lamp-post in Frith Street, went back to his office and waited for Sullivan to call. When he did, the news wasn't good.

'Lost them, I'm afraid.'

'What do you mean, lost them?'

'Well, we covered the place with a couple of men, watched you make the drop, but by the end of a couple of hours when nothing had happened they checked out the litter bin. The cupboard was bare.'

'Your men must have been incompetent.'

'Now, now, Mr McKechnie, that's a very slanderous thing to say. The streets were very busy – that's why the fellow chooses one o'clock – and my men can't exactly stand around in blue uniforms, you know. And I can't put my most experienced men on the job – their faces are too well known. That's the trouble with this patch.'

'So what do we do now?'

'We try again.'

'What about my hundred quid?'

'Oh, I'm sure you'll find a way to write that off, Mr McKechnie.' Why did everyone seem so certain that his losses were tax deductible? Were they trying to make it easier for him – or for themselves?

A fortnight later Salvatore called again; another drop was made, and another hundred lost as Sullivan's men failed to spot the pick-up, or were distracted for a few vital seconds, or, as McKechnie suggested down the phone, fell asleep.

'Now these slanderous suggestions won't help anyone, you know,' Sullivan said. He sounded formally apologetic about his men's failure, but not deeply unhappy.

McKechnie *was* deeply unhappy. He'd agreed to let Sullivan take over the case in the hope of getting some action. Since then, the file on the cutting of his wife had been moved from Guildford to West Central, and that was about all the action he'd had. He'd lost £250 in four weeks, no one knew who had attacked his wife, and Sullivan didn't seem to care. He couldn't even go and visit Sullivan because Salvatore or his mates were obviously following him, or had a spy somewhere; so all he could do was sit in his office by the telephone and wait for Sullivan to report the bad news to him.

It was when Sullivan lost him the third hundred that McKechnie decided on a new initiative. He called West Central and asked for Det-Sgt Shaw. He explained that he needed to see him urgently and privately; could they meet for a drink in the next day or two, but well away from their normal stamping ground? Shaw agreed.

They met at a drinkers' pub near Baker Street Station, a large, cheerless place where they never bothered to get rid of the fog of cigarette smoke between shifts; the drinkers relished it mainly because it was so murkily different from what they were going home to. They were going home to wives and children and cleanliness and their favourite dinner, so they valued the pub for its dirt and its smell and its maleness and its churlish refusal to go in for peanuts or crisps or new types of mixers or anything which might attract gaggles of typists after work and disturb their serious masculine drinking. Shaw often stopped off on his way home up the Metropolitan Line; McKechnie had never been here before.

'I want advice,' said McKechnie. 'I want you to listen to

me while I talk. I'll tell you everything that's happened to me, and if at the end you think you can't say anything without compromising yourself or your job, then I'll quite understand if you just down your drink and head for the door. All I ask is that you don't pass on what I tell you. Is that a deal?'

Shaw nodded. He was a small, foxy man, always too worried to smile. McKechnie told his story. When the name of Sullivan first cropped up, he thought he saw a slight twitch of a muscle on Shaw's face, but no more. When he had finished, Shaw lit a cigarette to add to the general fug, drew on it a few times, and then spoke without looking at McKechnie. It was as if he were avoiding responsibility for his words, as if McKechnie were simply overhearing him in a pub.

'Let's say that I appreciate your problem. Let's say that it could have happened before. Let's say that once a case is with an officer of a certain rank, it's not easy to get that case transferred except at the officer's own request. As a general rule. I'm naturally speaking in very general terms,' Shaw drew in another lungful, 'and it would be more than my job is worth to speculate on motives in individual cases.'

'Of course.'

'And nothing I say must be read as criticism of any officer.'

'Of course.' There was a long silence.

'If we were in America,' said McKechnie, 'I suppose I would go to a private detective.'

'You could do that here,' said Shaw, 'if you fancy hiring an active pensioner who once used to be good at catching couples on the job. They don't exist any more, and if they do, you might as well give your money straight to Oxfam as use them.'

'So what do I do if I don't want to go on paying out a hundred quid a fortnight for the rest of my life?'

'That's what I'm thinking about,' said Shaw. He tilted his empty glass towards his companion.

McKechnie got up and fetched them some more drinks. The pub was such a bastion of maleness that it didn't even have barmaids. A fat man in a striped shirt with beer stains down it served him with a convincing display of surliness. A few commuters were resignedly gathering up their raincoats and briefcases before heading off dejectedly towards sun and light and domestic bliss. McKechnie thought how, in comparison, he was quite happy with Rosie. Despite his occasional mistress, he was really fond of her. Her wouldn't want anything to happen to her. As he set down their drinks, Shaw said,

'You could try Duffy.'

'Who's that?'

'Duffy. Nick Duffy. Used to be a sort of buddy of mine. Did a couple of years in vice. Left the force, oh, about four years ago.'

'What does he do now?'

'He set up as a security adviser. Tells companies how to vet their staff, how to put their money in the safe, that sort of thing. Does the odd bit of freelancing; and he certainly knows the patch. He might do a job if he was free.'

'Why did he leave the police? Was he kicked out?'

'Let's say he left under a bit of a cloud.'

'Is he a criminal?'

Shaw looked up and smiled a wan, ironic smile.

'Well, we all have our own definitions of criminality, don't we? It's rather a big subject. But if you're asking me is he honest, then I'd say to you that Nick Duffy has got to be honest.'

'How do I get in touch with him?'

'He's in the book.'

'Well, thank you.'

'No, don't thank me. You don't thank me because you haven't seen me. O.K.? And two things. I didn't put you

38

on to Duffy: you've never heard of me, O.K.? And the other thing: it's probably not a good idea to ask Duffy why he left the force. He's a bit touchy on that score.'

Shaw left quickly, before McKechnie even had time to finish his drink.

3

The sunlight streaming in through the high window of the Paddington mews flat twinkled on the gold stud in Duffy's left ear. He'd sometimes dreamed of trying to invent a miniaturised alarm system, so that when the stud heated up a degree or two with the sun, a tiny bell went off in his ear. He'd given up the idea for two reasons: half the time he slept on his left side; and in any case, only a fool would rely on the sun.

Duffy had toyed with the idea in the first place because he hated clocks. He couldn't sleep if there were clocks in the place. He could hear a wrist watch from the other side of the room. An alarm clock always worked for him because its tick prevented him from getting to sleep in the first place. As he lived in a one-room flat ('open plan' was how the house agents dignified it), there was nowhere for clocks to go. The only timepieces allowed in had to be wrapped up. There was a Tupperware box in the bathroom marked 'Watches' for those who stayed the night. His kitchen clock was hung outside the kitchen window, in a polythene bag, its face pressing up against the glass. Sometimes, in the winters, birds would alight on it, thinking it was some sort of feeding apparatus, and peck inquisitively at the polythene. Then the bag would leak and Duffy would have to buy a new clock.

Duffy hated alarm clocks even more because they made him sweat when they went off; their tone seemed panicky, and this always got through to him before he was properly awake, so that he came into consciousness feeling anxious. It was never the right way to start the day. For the same reason, he hated alarm calls in the morning, and tried instead to train himself to wake up at a pre-determined time. Sometimes it worked, sometimes it didn't. It worked often enough to persuade him once to try leaving the telephone off the hook, so that he wouldn't be made anxious by some early morning call. But when he did, he found that all night the dialling tone roared at him across the room like a cageful of lions. Then he thought of buying a big soundproof box to put the telephone in at nights, but decided that if he started doing that he would end up crazy, living in a flat where everything that made a noise – telephone, radio, refrigerator, front door bell – was neatly boxed in. You just had to live with a certain level of anxiety, he reckoned.

So when the telephone went that morning he reacted normally – that is, he jumped as if the bailiffs had just booted in his front door. The girl beside him stirred and started shaking herself awake. Duffy was already across the room and standing naked at the telephone. He was a short, stockily built man with powerful forearms and haunches; he wore his hair in a longish brushcut which added perhaps an inch to his height. As he turned while talking on the phone, the girl ran her eyes over his slightly bowed legs, his cock, his pubic bush which was just catching the light, his chest with its concentration of dark hair round the nipples, his broad, strong face with a slightly small, tight mouth; she noticed a sudden flash from the stud in his left ear.

The girl sat up in bed and listened to Duffy's side of the conversation. It mainly consisted of pauses, grunts, 'nos' and 'all rights'. Duffy never said Yes. If he was with you and meant Yes, he'd nod his head. If he was on the phone, he'd say 'All right'. If you asked Duffy to marry you and he wanted to, he'd still only say 'All right'. She couldn't be completely sure, of course, but that was her guess. She'd once asked Duffy to marry her, and he'd said 'No'.

As Duffy put down the phone and walked back towards

41

the bed, she slightly turned towards him. She had a
pretty, circular Irish face, and cute, high breasts with
small dark brown nipples. She looked at Duffy's cock
nostalgically.

'Duffy,' she said, 'do you still remember what it was
like to fuck me?'

Duffy frowned.

'We've been into that,' he said, and walked away to the
bathroom. There he opened the Tupperware box marked
'Watches', saw from Carol's Timex that it was after ten,
washed, and started to lather his chin. From behind he
heard Carol's voice from the bed,

'I know we've been into it. I just wanted to know if you
used to like it.'

Duffy paused in his lathering, cleared his lips of soap
with the back of the little finger of his right hand, and
grunted back,

'All right.'

By the time he had finished in the bathroom, Carol had
already laid the breakfast at the round table at the other
end of the room. She sat wearing his blue towelling
dressing gown. He had put on the light, short kimono
which she always kept at the flat. It finished just below his
rump. He wore it quite a lot.

'Work?' she asked.

He nodded. 'Maybe.'

'Telling me about it?'

'No. Not until I've taken it or not taken it.'

'You need the money, Duffy.'

'I know.'

Duffy Security had had a pretty up-and-down three
years. Duffy had started up at a time when security was
already a booming business. Prospective clients could
look in the Yellow Pages and get a choice of any number
of firms; even with a display box round your name, you
were still competing with lots of better-known organis-

ations offering every sort of service – mobile patrols, cash transit, dog patrols, keyholders, static guards, personnel screening. Duffy didn't have a dog, though he did have a van; he also didn't have any staff apart from an answerphone and a friend who came in once a month to help with the accounts.

What Duffy did have was lots of expert knowledge and a highly practical mind. But you can't put that in an ad. People who want security naturally assume that the bigger the firm is, the better its operation. In fact, as Duffy knew only too well from his days in the force, the large firms were always being infiltrated by ex-cons and stoolies; a hundred quid in the right place could buy you a lot of information if you were in the business of knocking off cash transfers.

The only way to get successful in this field, Duffy knew, was to work at being really efficient and then hope for word-of-mouth to back you up. You couldn't advertise in any effective way. Or rather, there might be ways, but they just weren't feasible. One would be to have a variety of crooks who'd been nabbed as a result of one of your systems quoted saying things like, 'I'd still be out there nicking if it hadn't been for DUFFY SECURITY'. But even old lags have their pride. The other way would be to get firms you had advised to endorse you: 'We've never had a break-in since we called in DUFFY SECURITY'. But anything like that would just seem an open challenge to every operator in town.

So Duffy checked out his answerphone every day, took most of the jobs that were offered, and just about kept going. He wasn't sure about the job this fellow McKechnie was offering; but he'd meet the guy at least. He said,

'What time's your shift?'

'Three. Three to eleven.' It was the shift Carol disliked the most. Nothing much happened all through the afternoon and early evening, and then, as soon as you were really tired, you were likely to get a bit of trouble on your hands.

'Ah, the old shit shift.'

Duffy got up from the table and walked to his fitted wardrobe at the other end of the room. A stranger would have thought his flat a bit empty. Duffy thought his flat a bit empty too. It had been like that since the second robbery.

The first time he was robbed they only took the television set and his electric razor. It had been more of an embarrassment than anything else, especially the one-inch para in the *Evening Standard* headed 'SECURITY MAN ROBBED'. He'd been wanting to get a new T.V. anyway; and, just to prove to the thieves that he didn't really miss anything, he went back to wet shaving.

The second time he was robbed they had come back for everything else: they arrived in a van marked Handimoves, took his furniture, his electric cooker, his fireside rug, his radio, his new television, his electric kettle, his pile of sixpences and even a pot plant. All they left were his fitted carpet, the ashtrays, and his bed. Why hadn't they taken the bed?

The first thing Duffy had done on this occasion was ring the news desk on the *Standard* and speak to an old mate of his. He bartered the story of the break-in – which was bound to reach them sooner or later – for a small case of drunken driving by a judge which he'd heard about a couple of days earlier and which was being quietly hushed. Only then did he call the police and get ready for their cracks when he told them what he did for a living.

In fact, Duffy didn't really mind the robberies. He quite liked buying new furniture, and the insurance company had paid up on both occasions without any quibbles. Moreover, Duffy always maintained that insurance was the best form of security. When he first started advising people about how to protect their homes and offices, he used to tell them that there were four systems to choose from. The best was total, comprehensive, wall-to-wall insurance. The second was a complex network of electronic beams and scanners so sensitive that it triggered when the night watchman farted. The third was your average burglar alarm, of the sort which thieves practise dismantling with their eyes closed just to keep in trim. And the fourth was a white plywood box; painted on it in red were the words DUFFY SECURITY, a miniature skull and a ragged flash of lightning. You attached a few fake wires to it and stuck it high up on the front of your house. In terms of cost-effectiveness Duffy used to recommend the fourth system: until, that is, the funny look in clients' eyes began to make him realise that they didn't want to hear the truth: they wanted to be told what they wanted to be told. From then on, that was what he told them.

'Will I see you tonight?' He asked the question in a deliberately casual way.

'Oh, I don't think so, Duffy. Not two nights on the trot. That would be just a bit too much like old times, wouldn't it?'

'All right. See you then.'

'See you.'

Duffy pulled on a green suede blouson with a big plastic zip up the front, and left Carol to finish breakfast by herself.

He reached McKechnie's Rupert Street office by half past eleven. Between a shuttered dirty bookshop and a twenty-four-hour minicab service he found a doorway; a couple of grubby plastic strips screwed to the side wall announced WORLDWIDE PRODUCTIONS (LONDON) INC. and MCKECHNIE IMPORTS. He walked up to the first floor, pushed open a door and saw a plain secretary wearing a long skirt and a big silver cross; she was reading a magazine. She did the full secretarial college number on

45

him, but her face said that his arrival in the office was a high point in the day. Visitors were clearly as rare and fascinating as white men at the source of the Limpopo.

'Mr McKechnie is just a little bit tied up at the moment, but I'll see when he'll be free,' she said.

'He said eleven thirty,' said Duffy. 'It's eleven thirty. If he's busy then I'm buggering off.'

'Oh, I'm sure he'll be able to fit you in,' she smiled, and buzzed the telephone. 'Mr McKechnie, we have a Mr Duffy to see you in reception. Thank you, Mr McKechnie. Mr Duffy, would you go through, please, it's that door there.'

Duffy looked round the secretary's office. It was about the size of a broom cupboard, filled with box files and steel cabinets. There were only two doors – the one he had come in through and another opposite. Maybe there were a few customers who thought McKechnie had his office out on the stairs or something. As he put his hand on the knob he looked round the secretary's room again.

'Is this reception?'

She smiled and nodded.

'Just checking.'

McKechnie rose to shake hands with Duffy. He was a bit surprised how short the security man was, but he looked quite strong. He also looked a bit of a faggot to McKechnie's eye. He wondered about that gold stud in his ear. Was it just fashion, or was it some sort of sexual signal? McKechnie didn't know any more. In the old days, you knew precisely where you were: all the codes were worked out, you could tell who did and who didn't, who was and who wasn't. Even a few years ago you could still not go wildly wrong; but nowadays the only way of being quite sure who was what and who did what was when you asked your secretary to clean your glasses and she took off her knickers to do it with.

Duffy reserved judgment on McKechnie. So far he was

46

just another client – just another red-faced middle-aged man who might or might not be honest, might or might not be just after some free advice, might or might not be wasting his at the moment not very valuable time. He listened while McKechnie told him the first part of the story, the part to do with the break-in; McKechnie was relieved that Duffy didn't smirk when he told him about the cat. Actually, Duffy thought it was quite funny – he'd seen so many nasty things happen to humans that he didn't have much space left over for animals – but he refrained from laughing because at the moment he needed almost every customer he could get. Then McKechnie told him about Sullivan and West Central and the three hundred and fifty quid. He waited for comments.

'So why did you come to me?'

'I asked around.'

At least he hadn't said he'd picked Duffy's name out of the Yellow Pages with a pin.

'And what do you expect me to do?'

'I don't know yet. I want to hear what you say first.'

'Well, I'd say you've got two problems, maybe separate, possibly connected. First, what happened at your house and the phone calls. I must say I hadn't thought of doing the presh that way round before. It's quite clever.'

'What do you mean?'

'Well, normally what happens with presh is that they send a heavy man round who tells you the fee and the delivery date, and then tells you what they'll do to you if you don't deliver – set fire to your house, kill your dog, kidnap your kid, or whatever. You think about it and then usually you do what they ask. And then maybe, after a while, after a few deliveries, you don't pay, and they decide to sort you out, except that you're expecting them to do that and so you might just have the blues there or *something*. But this way round, they do the rough stuff

47

first, when no one can possibly be expecting it, let the customer stew, and then put in for the fee. It's a different system, it's not so predictable, and it throws in an extra element of craziness. The customer – you in this case – thinks, Christ, well, if they cut my wife before I hadn't even not done something they asked, what the hell would they be like to mess with if I *had* done something they didn't like; for instance, if I hadn't paid up. So their first bit of heavy takes them coasting a long way, you see.'

'I do. And who do you think this Salvatore is?'

'No idea. I knew the old Salvatore a bit. You used to see him in Italian restaurants trying to look like a mafioso. Used to walk in, sit down, not say a word, eat his food, drink his wine, get up, walk out. Very dignified, slightly sinister, dressed in black, had a pepper-and-salt moustache. All the other diners thought he must be a big protection man. Well, he was a medium-sized protection man; did a few smokes and tarts as well, I think. Some of the restaurants he really did have the screw on; but the others, well, he just had a slate there and they used to send him the bill at the end of the month. And he always paid. He was a humorous old bugger, that's for sure; quite a character. It sounds as if this bloke knew him, or maybe inherited a bit of his patch; or maybe he just liked his style. He sounds as if he's got a bit of a sense of humour from what you say.'

'Well, it's the sort of humour which appeals to him more than me. So what about the second part of it?'

'Hard to say. Could be anywhere on the scale from straight incompetence up to a lot of bent. I can't imagine the blues losing three drops in a row. Not unless standards have fallen since I was there. But quite what it means is another matter. This guy at West Central might simply be telling you he doesn't need the business: hasn't got the time, hasn't got the men, doesn't care enough about your problems.'

'I didn't know the police could do that.'

'Not in theory they can't. They've got a duty to investigate. But they've also got practical problems. They naturally spend most of the time going for the big stuff and only go for the little stuff when there's a good chance of an arrest.'

'So this is little? My wife has thirteen stitches and I'm paying out a hundred quid a fortnight?'

'Well, Mr McKechnie, there's big and big. And there are a couple of other possibilities.'

'Which are?'

'That the bloke at West Central is keeping tabs on what's going on but thinks it's too early to come in. He's waiting for it all to blow up like a great boil full of pus, and then he'll come in and burst it. Some people call this the romantic approach to police work. Some people call it the lazy approach. And then of course . . .' Duffy paused.

'Yes?'

'There's another possibility. This guy . . .'

'Sullivan?'

'Yes, Sullivan – he may be thinking that it's all a private business anyway; that it's just a little squabble about a patch. What about that, Mr McKechnie?'

'What do you mean?'

'Well, I don't know anything about you. As far as I know, you're a perfectly normal trader who deals in funny hats or whatever. But, of course, if you had form, that might be different . . .'

'Form?'

'You haven't got a criminal record, I hope, Mr McKechnie?'

'I hope so too. No, of course I don't.'

'Good. Well, then, there's only the last possibility, which wouldn't be the easiest one for either of us. That this guy Sullivan is in direct collusion with whoever is using Salvatore's name.'

49

'And what would you do if that were the case?'

'I'd advise you to sell up as fast as you can and get your tail out of the area, Mr McKechnie. An expanding operator and a sleeping policeman are a very unpleasant combination to come across.'

'But we don't by any means know that, do we, Mr Duffy?'

'No, fortunately, we don't.'

'And in the meantime?'

'In the meantime I can do some scouting about for you. I don't think I – or you for that matter – want to get too near the second area of concern. If you're dealing with a bent copper, the only rule I know is, stay away.'

'And what about the first area?'

'Well, we haven't got much to start on. We've got a short man and a tall one at your home, one of them with a Stanley knife. No prints. One of them a bit sick by the sound of it. We've got a fat bloke with glasses and ginger hair just off Shaftesbury Avenue. And we've got a voice down the phone. What sort of a voice, Mr McKechnie?'

'Quite deep. He started off a bit Italian; now he's got more English, but possibly not quite English. Sometimes has what sounds like a slight accent, sometimes puts his words in a funny order. No, that's not quite right, but he did start off saying lots of things like "As you say" or "How do you put it?".'

'Doesn't tell us much. If he gets a kick out of pretending to be Salvatore, maybe he likes putting on a bit of an Italian accent as well. I'll fix a tape on your phone as soon as I can.'

'So what do we do next, Mr Duffy?'

'We wait for you to get your next orders. And then we see what they are. And then we decide what to do. In the meanwhile I'll mooch around and see what I can pick up. I'll come back tomorrow and fix your phone; but after that we'd better not meet here again, just in case you're being watched. We'll keep in touch by phone.'

They bargained briefly about money. Duffy asked for thirty a day, and settled for twenty (however long the day was), or three quid an hour for part of a day, plus tube fares and any goods he bought for which he could produce a receipt. Then he asked for a silly hat and a mask.

'I don't think our sort of masks will make you a master of disguise, Mr Duffy.'

'It's just to have in my hand as I leave, in case you're being watched. Makes me look more like a potential customer who's been given some samples.'

'Very true, Mr Duffy. Shall I invoice you for them?'

'Yes, please.'

McKechnie wrote out an invoice. With a smile, Duffy handed it straight back to him. 'Expenses receipt,' he said, and left. He walked out into Rupert Street with a cone-shaped clown's hat in one hand and a King Kong mask with plastic hair in the other. Two Cypriot youths were loitering at the entrance to the minicab office and an unhealthily pale man was taking down the wire shutters on the window of the dirty bookshop. It was beginning to cloud over.

McKechnie had lied to Duffy about his bit of trouble with the law. Duffy, on the other hand, had lied to McKechnie by pretending not to register Sullivan's name. He knew Sullivan. He knew Sullivan from way back. And the memory of him tugged with it all those other memories which he normally kept locked away at the back of his skull, and which only escaped by chance, or when Carol said something to him like she'd said that morning.

Duffy knew more than just Sullivan. He knew West Central like the back of his hand. He'd been a detective-sergeant there for three years before the thing happened which finished his career. He'd done a year's general there, and two years' vice. He'd loved the work; he'd had a good giggle with the rest of the lads at the Xmas blue film shows; he'd got to know the patch and the whores, and made friends with a few of them; he'd known who handled smokes, who handled snort and who handled smack; he'd got an inkling of how the tight, impenetrable Chinese community ran itself – of when they ceremoniously deferred to white law, and when they didn't give a wine waiter's cork about it – and he'd learnt all about presh. He was on his way to becoming one of the best officers on the patch. Not just that, but one of the happiest too: when a pretty, round-faced, dark-haired, Irish-looking W.P.C. had joined them, there'd been the usual stampede from his colleagues. He'd hung back a bit, waited for the dust to die down, and then got talking to her. She got talking back, and they were away. Things couldn't have been working out better.

What wrecked it all were two things: honesty and sex. Duffy, like most coppers, had a slightly flexible approach to the truth. You had to if you wanted to survive: not survive as a copper, but survive within yourself. The zealots who saw truth as indivisible ended up in either A10 or the cuckoo farm. Most of the time you stuck to the truth as closely as you could, but were prepared to bend with the breeze if necessary. Sometimes, for instance, it might be necessary to tell a little lie, fiddle your notebook just a bit, in order to make sure that a much bigger lie didn't get to pass itself off as the truth. On those occasions you felt bad for a bit, though you knew you didn't have any choice in the matter.

But Duffy, like most coppers, knew that you always drew a line somewhere. You might tidy up your verbals a bit, fiddle your evidence slightly, forget a little something, but you always knew why you were doing it: you were fixing the record in favour of justice. You weren't doing it to get promotion, you weren't doing it to get your own back on a villain for personal reasons, and you weren't doing it because you were on the take.

That was the way it normally was, the way it was for most coppers. But not for all. Some coppers were bent as corkscrews, and they didn't last long. The tricky ones were the half-and-halfers. Sullivan, for instance. You could never be quite sure about the Super. He always kept his own company, always seemed a bit lazy, a bit bored; he turned in a good enough arrest record, yet always seemed to be keeping some of himself in reserve. Partly it was that he'd been at the station longer than anyone else. He'd say things like 'My experience tells me, lad . . . ' and 'When you've been around West Central as long as I have . . . ' and 'Listen, my boy, I was charging Jasmine when you still didn't know what your middle leg was for . . . ' Most of the younger men tried to look on him as an avuncular figure, but none quite succeeded.

One summer a couple of new whores had started operating from a gaff on the corner of Bateman Street and Frith. One was a black kid, the other white, and they worked as a pair when they street-hustled. There wasn't that much street-work going on – at least not in broad daylight; but these two were new to the patch, and they either had a brash approach to the market or else were run by a very grabby pimp, so they often hustled the street. One would keep a lookout and the other would proposition a prick. If he didn't walk off at once, but couldn't quite make up his mind, she'd point to her lookout and say, 'Maybe you like my friend?' The hesitating punter felt flattered at being given a choice, and thinking it almost impolite to refuse both of them, would make his selection. Duffy saw them work this trick lots of times.

They had looked like a couple of tough-faced twenty-year-olds who could take care of themselves. But they cut just as easily as anybody else. One evening in Bateman Street someone stuck a knife into the black girl, first into her shoulder and then, as she was falling, into her rump, as near to her cunt as he could. The girl lay in the gutter and bled a lot; and then she was taken to hospital where she was stitched up. She told Duffy she'd cut herself opening a tin of baked beans.

Stabbing at the cunt is the way pimps warn other pimps off their patch. You don't cut the pimp, who might fight back, you cut one of his girls. Duffy wasn't sentimental about whores, but he didn't much like that sort of crime, and on this occasion he got a bit tough. He leaned on Polly, as the black girl called herself, for the name of her pimp. Then he went to the pimp and leaned a bit harder on him. Then he got a lead on someone called Savella who'd tried to warn off the pimp a few times in the weeks before the attack.

He started to lean on Savella, which was a lot harder than leaning on the pimp because Savella was a whole deal smarter and had a bright villain's grounding in the law. Duffy went to see him a few times and made a nuisance of himself. He played it like one enthusiastic copper. He asked who Savella worked for. Savella wouldn't tell him – 'Amma self-ampaloyed' he kept repeating – but Duffy went on asking around. Finally, he came up with a name: Big Eddy. No other name, no description. He carried on asking. He was keen on his case.

Eventually, Sullivan called him in.

'Not getting very far with this stabbing, Duffy.'

Duffy begged to disagree. He'd got to the pimp, he'd got to Savella, he'd got to the name of Big Eddy. He'd made a few new contacts. The girls might talk more. He thought he'd got hold of someone who might have something he could use to put pressure on Savella.

'My experience tells me the case is folding,' said Sullivan.

Again, Duffy begged to differ. Anyway, he'd carried on in the past with much less to go on than he had now.

'I repeat,' said Sullivan, fixing Duffy with a couple of

small toad-like eyes, the only live portions of his flabby, inanimate face, 'that my experience tells me the case is folding.'

Duffy knew at the time that this was one occasion when he should bend with the breeze, one of those times when you shrug and say, 'It's only a whore' – and, in this case, not a particularly nice one either. Foolishly, he didn't. He went on with the case. He wasn't exactly in breach of police regulations because Sullivan hadn't officially closed the case, or taken it over, or handed it to someone else. It was just that in every other respect Sullivan had told him to lay off.

He'd just got a fresh line on Big Eddy when the rug was pulled. Quite how it happened and who was the stool he never knew, but there must have been a tip from someone inside the station. Everyone there knew he'd been going through a sticky time with Carol. They'd had one of those spells everyone gets after a year or so of knowing each other, when the freshness has worn off a bit and everyone starts treating you as an established couple and whistling the Wedding March at you and doing cradling gestures and you suddenly wonder whether you're doing the right thing after all. You want to stand back, think about it a bit, make sure you're on the right path. Duffy had tried to explain this to Carol, who'd assumed he was trying to drop her in as painless a way as possible. She wasn't going to be dropped like that by anyone. She yelled and she cried and he told her she was jumping to the wrong conclusions but that her acting like this was anyway proving that she was assuming things which they hadn't ever discussed, and that of course he still loved her, but she really ought to try and see the relationship from another angle. Like his, for instance, she said.

Eventually they agreed on a couple of months apart, no strings, no bed, no conditions; then they'd see how they felt.

After about three weeks Duffy started getting pretty itchy. They'd agreed not to impose anything on each other for the two months: they could be as free as they liked. Duffy debated with himself about what to do, and then gave in.

The point about Duffy was, as McKechnie surmised, that he plugged in both ways. He didn't need a transformer. He'd had a very gay phase when he was eighteen, then sobered up a lot when he joined the force, and since then pretty well divided his favours equally between the two sexes. His mates at work saw he was keen enough on women for them not to suspect him; the other half of his preference he kept more or less to himself. He told Carol, who merely said she'd always thought that she had a rather boyish body, and asked if he'd like her to dress up as a bloke from time to time. He said it wasn't exactly like that; but he was pleased at the way she reacted.

When they took their two months' separation from each other and Duffy got itchy, he thought a lot about which way to go. If he went for a girl, Carol would be bound to be jealous, despite the agreement. If he went for a guy, then maybe she'd feel he was – what would she say? – slipping backwards; but maybe she wouldn't feel so threatened when he told her. In terms of sexual pleasure, it didn't make much difference to him; he wasn't picky when it came to orgasm.

The first time he went trawling at the Caramel Club and took a chubby journalist back to the flat he was then living in off Westbourne Grove. A couple of nights later he went to the Alligator and landed himself a polite undergraduate hot off the Oxford train. The third time he went back to the Caramel again, drank a bit more than usual, and was half-helped home by a nice black kid of about his own age.

Ten minutes after that his flat door was kicked in by two full-sized policemen, the black kid started yelling, 'He bought me drinks, he bought me drinks,' and the larger of the two policemen seized him by the bare shoulder, twisted him round on the bed and said, with heavy irony, 'Excuse me, sir, but how old is your friend?' The whisky fumes were clearing from his head as if someone had switched on an Xpelair, and he knew he'd been set up.

The kid was a plant; he said he was nineteen. The police took an address and told him to scram. They took Duffy down to the station and charged him. When he told them his profession, one of the two policemen turned his back while the other punched Duffy in the kidneys. 'Fucking bent queer copper,' he said; then 'Fucking *queer*,' and punched him again.

Duffy knew it was curtains. He was suspended from duty and sat around gloomily at home. Eventually he was called to West Central. And who should give him the good news but Sullivan?

'When you've been around as long as I have, nothing much surprises you, Duffy. But this does. This does. I've argued for you, though personally my instinct would be to throw everything at you. I've talked to the investigating officer in the case and I've got you the best deal I can; a sight better than you deserve. And I've done it not for your sake but for the sake of the station, I don't mind telling you. Westbourne Grove have agreed not to prosecute; they'll say it might cause the kid too much psychological harm to give evidence and they're writing the case off. Now go away and come back in five minutes with your resignation.'

It was a perfect fit-up. It destroyed his career, and it wrecked his relationship with Carol. Moreover, Duffy failed to appreciate Sullivan's avuncular touch when he called Carol into his office to explain what had happened. She had stayed away from Duffy for two months, trying to understand what had happened. When she came to see him, he did his best to explain, but there were too many scars. They tried going to bed together to see what that would do, but she was tense and nervy and he couldn't get a hard-on. Sleeping was all right, though, and waking up together was usually nice. Gradually they got back together a bit, but only as wary friends. Sometimes Carol stayed the night, but they never made advances to each other in bed. He never got a hard-on when she was in bed with him, not even a sleepy, unintended one.

'Brother and sister?' she'd once said to him as they were falling asleep. Brother and sister, but with a suspicious loitering past. Brother and sister with a lot of previous.

Duffy had good reason to remember Sullivan.

4

Duffy woke up out of a bad dream. It was a bad dream because for Duffy life within it was all fivers and éclairs. In his dream he was a Chief Super in whose presence villains shrank to the size of earwigs; he snapped his fingers and cases on which the brightest blues had broken their teeth simply fell open in his hands. After a triumphant day at the office like this he was driven home to a large detached house deep in some beech woods where Carol and the kids were waiting for him. As he drove through the gates his eldest son, a flaxen-haired rascal, fired his bow and arrow at the car; the rubber sucker on the end of the arrow glued itself to the hub-cap and the car rolled along like Boadicea's chariot, slicing the heads off bluebells all the way up the drive. No matter, Duffy thought in his dream, the bluebells will never run out. Then they got to the house and Carol was waiting on the steps. As they stepped inside the door, she gently tugged on his sleeve and took him upstairs. She slipped off her dress and was wearing nothing underneath. Duffy threw his suit over a chair, climbed out of the rest of his clothes, and as he approached the bed where she lay on top of the candlewick cover she exclaimed, as if surprised by joy, 'Duffy, you're so big, you're so big.'

'AAAAAAaaaaaaaaaaaaaaaaaaaaaaahhhhhhhhhh . . . ' He screamed himself awake. It was one of those dreams when you know all the time you're dreaming. Usually they're bad dreams, and you comfort yourself with the knowledge that your brain is just having a mean time with you. But when you're in a good dream and know that it's only a dream, then you feel an undercurrent of bitterness all the way through and you wake with ashes in your mouth and strange pains and an unconquerable sense of loss. You feel as if America has slipped through your fingers.

Duffy lay on his back shaking a little. Out of curiosity, he lifted the bedclothes to see if he had a hard-on. No dice. Even if he dreamed he had a hard-on with Carol, even if he was fucking her in his dream, he awoke to a peeled prawn and a walnut. No dice.

Duffy wasn't impotent. He couldn't lay that at the door of whoever fitted him up. He was just impotent with Carol. At first he'd thought it was the shock of what had happened. Then he began to realise that he might get over the shock and still not recover his powers with her. Perhaps never. He'd tried lying in bed with her and ordering his cock to obey, silently shouting and cursing it. He'd tried closing his eyes and thinking of other women he'd fucked, and other men he'd fucked, and the most exciting pornography he'd ever clapped eyes on. No dice. Desperate, he'd even tried wanking himself to erection and then turning towards Carol; but his cock, unruly to the bitter end, wilted like a flower at dusk. No dice.

And the end *was* bitter. If you can't fuck the one person you want to fuck, then pleasure got from fucking other people is even more lined with irony. After a while, at Carol's insistence, he went off and tried fucking other people. To his distress, there was no problem; to his further distress, he always found himself enjoying it just enough to want to do it again. He fucked men and women indiscriminately, but found that, without realising he was doing it, he was setting himself a rule: never twice. The sweetest girl, the randiest guy, both would leave in the morning. However much they asked to see him again, and however nice he thought they were, he would never say 'All right'. Never. It was, perhaps, a sort of fidelity to Carol, even if a fidelity wrung from the most fevered promiscuity.

What Carol did he never asked. He didn't ask because all the answers she could give were bad. If she was sleeping with lots of guys, he knew he'd hate it; if she was sleeping with just one guy, he'd hate it more; if she was sleeping with no one, he'd hate it less but feel the pressure on him even more intolerable. Duffy, in short, was in a state of pain.

It's a state for which the only cure is work. Duffy had mixed feelings about McKechnie's job. It might increase the pain inside him to go back prowling round his old patch; maybe it would just stir everything up and never give him the chance to come to terms with it. On the other hand, maybe there would be some opportunity of making a settlement with his past. But what if there were, and he muffed it?

Still, it was work, it would get him out of his flat some mornings. It was twenty quid a day plus tube fares. Duffy could do with that. The bars he cruised had suddenly put up their prices a lot. People said it was the one pleasure that was free, but it wasn't. You had to pay one way or the other: either with your feelings, or else in buying drinks as you tested the company, weighed it up, went through the social rituals which were essential if you wanted to end up not feeling a complete whore.

Duffy dug out his basic electrician's kit from a cupboard and set off for Rupert Street. He'd already told McKechnie to bring in a small tape recorder and a number of tapes. At the office they sent Belinda out for a couple of take-away coffees and Duffy pressed a rubber sucker on to the body of the telephone on McKechnie's desk. A short length of wiring connected it to the portable Sony in the top drawer.

'Secret Service stuff, eh?' said McKechnie, who was getting quite excited.

'This is Cubs' stuff,' replied Duffy. 'Put me up to thirty a day and I'll get you free calls to Australia.'

'We're not quite *that* big yet. What about Barnsley?'

'It's harder to fix than Australia, funnily enough. Cost you forty.'

'You're a hard man, Duffy.' Duffy winced. McKechnie must have heard that line somewhere and thought it was the thing to say.

'Now, it's quite simple. When Salvatore comes on the line, you just press the Record button in the normal way. And don't forget to talk natural.'

'What do I do with the tape?'

'Call me afterwards and I'll tell you what to do. I won't come and collect it. Maybe I'll work out a drop. Or you could always post it.' The last suggestion sounded rather limp, even if it probably was the most efficient. Duffy constantly found that clients expected all sorts of secret tricks for their money. They wanted you to use a walkie-talkie when it was easier to use a public callbox; they wanted the windows of your car to be all blacked out although this made you the most conspicuous vehicle on the road; they wanted to leave things for you behind lavatory cisterns and wear false moustaches and buy complicated telephoto lenses which they couldn't work. The last thing they wanted to see you doing was sitting on your butt, applying your brain to their particular problem, and coming up with a one-word solution. And the last thing of all they ever wanted to be told was, 'I should go to the police if I were you.' They hated that. Clients, Duffy reflected, were dumb.

Duffy turned down the offer of a second King Kong mask (he couldn't be bothered to take one, but what he actually said, to boost customer morale, was, 'No, it's a better disguise *not* to have one this time'), and stepped out into Rupert Street. The pale man who ran the dirty book-shop had just taken down his shutters and was fiddling with the neon sign in the window. So far it only read BOO.

Duffy took a breath, headed up to Shaftesbury Avenue, crossed it, and found himself back on the patch he'd worked for three years. He'd been back a few times, to a restaurant or something, but always in the evening, under cover of dark. Now he felt more unprotected, more recognisable. He dived into a coffee bar. Sitting over a *cappuccino*, he gave himself bottle. Four years was a long time: whores change, villains change, the blues change. If that was bad in terms of finding things out, it was good in terms of not being recognised. Besides, he looked different now. Before, it had been two-piece suits from Burton's and Hepworth's, with a sports jacket for when he was trying to look casual. Now it was Jean Junction, street markets, suede and leather, faded denim; his hair was quite a bit longer at the sides, and brush-cut on top; sometimes he wore shades with pale yellow glass in them.

And on top of that, the answer was to walk like a punter. Punters had two ways of walking – very fast, as if they had a couple of minutes to catch a train and couldn't get out of the Golden Mile quick enough, and very slow, as if they were killing time before an appointment, and that was the only reason they were loitering through the place. And whichever method they adopted, they always walked with their heads a bit down; they didn't look people in the face, and they believed, if they kept their eyes lowered, that no one could see if they were squinting sideways into the windows of dirty bookshops. The people who walked at a normal pace with their heads up, and who looked other people in the eye as they passed them, were the people who owned the place: the shopkeepers, the whores, the pimps, the restaurateurs, the villains, and the blues.

As a copper, Duffy had been street-wise. He knew the way the place worked, how to get around in it, where the skeins of power ran. You picked it up slowly, partly from other coppers, but just as importantly by finding out for yourself; by getting to know the patch not just physically, but somehow emotionally as well. You sensed it pulsing away. This wasn't the main part of being a copper: you didn't stand in the middle of Soho, mystically sniffing the air like Maigret, and then head off and run a villain to ground. It was just background; it was knowing where you were. But to Duffy it was a vital preliminary to the job.

He finished his coffee and went out to get the feel again of his old patch. He walked along Old Compton Street, up Greek, down Frith, up Dean, across little courts and alleys into D'Arblay, down into Broadwick (past West Central on the other side of the street), down into Brewer, along to where it nearly joins up with Berwick in a fetid knot of street markets and escort agencies and cinemas, past Raymond's Revuebar and back across into Dean. He ate a lasagne and green salad in a corner café, and reflected that he still had almost eighteen quid left for the day (McKechnie, after some protest, had paid him seventy-five pounds in advance).

In four years it had changed a bit to his eyes. There were more bookshops than before, and more sex shops with rubber cucumbers in the window. Massage parlours seemed to be holding steady. Strip clubs were a bit on the decline, and had largely given way to porno cinemas. A few years ago Soho simply had normal cinemas, but showing naughtier films from the regular distributors: *Danish Dentist on the Job, Nurse Call, Catch 69, Vixens Behind Barbed Wire*, those sort of films. If you wanted something a couple of degrees hotter, the only place to go was the Compton Cinema Club in Old Compton Street; and if after that you were still unsatisfied, as you came out there might, if you were lucky, be a tout or two on the pavement offering you a really blue film. Now, though, there were whole series of cinema clubs, called Triple-X and X-Citing and Double Blue and Eros Eyrie and Taboo, with gaudy signs outside offering XXX-rated movies to those over eighteen.

The heat of the early afternoon made Duffy feel, not exactly randy, but definitely a bit interested. Head down, he turned into a dirty bookshop on the corner of Greek Street. At the desk a Mediterranean youth was reading the racing news and watching over the small shelf of dirty movies. On two sides of the shop were racks of mags, arranged by customer interest. The largest section was the Hetero one; then came Homo; then Leather and S & M and Bondage and Big Tits and Schoolgirls; finally a few shelves of paperbacks. The sales technique of the shops hadn't changed: you left English mags open for browsers to see – let them get turned on by *Rustler* and *Rapier* and *Playbirds* and *Lovebirds* and *New Directions* and *QT* – but sealed up the more expensive American imports so that they looked as if they must be a lot hornier. Duffy smiled at the hopeless self-deceiving gamble which the punters continued to go in for, still trusting in a hot cover, an inflated price and a polythene bag. He glanced at the rack of Big Tit mags, whose publishers had always seemed to work harder at the titles of their mags. *D-Cup* was still going strong, he noted, and so was *42-Plus*; *Bazooms* was there too, making tits sound like ballistic missiles; and a new one called *Milkmaids*. Duffy remembered one that had started up a few years ago called *Charlies' Aunts*, which had tickled him at the time; it had folded after a couple of issues – the punters probably thought it contained beaver-shots of old ladies. Maybe the invention had gone out of the industry, he reflected.

Next to the Bondage section – a few copies of *Hogtie* and one or two of *All Roped Up* – was a doorway leading to some cubicles. 10p X-RATED PORNO MINI-MOVIES CHANGE AT DESK read the sign. This was something new since he'd been around. He got some change at the desk and went into one of the cubicles; pinned to the door was a torn-off box lid advertising the film he could see there: 'LESBO LOVERS – Two girls all alone and left to their own vices go horse riding and find lots going on underneath!!!'

Duffy sat down on the bench and fumbled with his change. There was no lock on the door, which you kept shut with an extended foot while you watched the film being projected on to a white board on the back of the door. Duffy kicked the door to, and then couldn't see where to put his money in. He opened the door again and found a metal box near his right hand. 10p and the film began. A large black girl sat in a bath and soaped herself, concentrating on her pubes and her tits. The film stopped. 10p and the girl took the shower attachment and hosed off her tits, then hosed off her pubes, rolling her eyes back as she did so. The film was a bit out of focus, but it might get more interesting as it went on, Duffy thought. Where were the other girl and the horse? 10p and the girl was in the bath still, soaping her tits and pubes again. Whether the film was being long-winded, or whether it had come to an end with his second 10p and was starting again, Duffy couldn't quite make out. His concentration began to wander. The light from the projector showed up the comments which previous punters had scrawled on the 'screen': NO FUCKING GOOD one of them had written, and another, ALLIE'S ARMY.

As he came out of the booth, Duffy's heel slipped a bit on the floor. With a pile of change still in his hand, he tried another cubicle. This time there were two girls, kissing each other rather demurely. 10p and they started rubbing each other's tits as if they were polishing silver. Duffy wondered – was it worth risking another 10p? Well, it's on McKechnie, he thought. 10p and the girls started stroking one another's pubes and acted opening their mouths in delight and surprise. The focus was better in this booth, and Duffy found his cock was quite enjoying the show. 10p and one of the girls was lying on top of the other. That wasn't so much fun. 10p and a skinny bloke with a moustache jumped out of the shower and the girls

66

acted 'Eeeek!' 10p and the skinny bloke started smacking their bottoms. There was no fun at all now; his cock told him it had had enough.

As he came out of the bookshop a girl jumped towards him. She was a plump, clean-looking girl with round, gold-rimmed glasses. She stood in front of him and pinned a badge onto his lapel. He squinted down and saw that it read 'Have a Happy Day'. She chirruped,

'We're trying to help poor children all over the world. I'm sure you'd like to make us a donation.'

She was bright in manner, polite, and firm. You couldn't take objection to her. Duffy could. Fucking Moonies, he thought, can't even leave the poor old guilt-ridden punters alone. He unpinned the badge and offered it back to her; she was already pulling out a record from her shoulder-bag,

'We're trying to help poor children. I'm sure you want to make a donation,' she repeated.

Duffy couldn't help saying what he thought. 'Fucking Moonie,' he said, dropped the badge and turned away. As he went she hit him over the head with the record.

That was new too, then, he reflected. He walked on down the street past a few Triple-X porno-blue clubs (he'd save them for another day), and came across something else that was new. PEEP SHOW, it said, LIVE GIRLS DANCE NUDE WHILE YOU WATCH. As he approached the place, head slightly down, he squinted sideways: 50p, the sign said, and DIFFERENT GIRLS. He walked on, then did a classic punter's double-back, putting on speed and suddenly jumping through the door. He changed a couple of quid at the desk and went into a tiny cell. The lock just about stopped the door from swinging open. At eye-level in the opposite wall there was an opening about the size of a letter box. On the floor were Kleenex tissues; some of them were damp. Disco music was being played on a powerful sound system.

Duffy dropped a 50p into the slot and a metal shutter at the level of his face jerked up, revealing a glass slit window. He pressed his nose against the glass and saw a girl dancing. The booths formed an almost complete circle round her, with a gap for her to come on and off stage. She was naked, thinnish, with a noticeable appendix scar and breasts which had probably been siliconed. She played with her tits and rubbed her pubes while dancing, and kept an eye on the row of slits, moving to face each new one that opened for a few seconds. Duffy laid out another 50p on her, though some of the time he spent looking round at the other letter boxes, at the anonymous pairs of eyes.

He'd had about 40p worth of the girl when the music suddenly stopped and she ran off stage. At once the next girl ran on, shedding her track suit as she came. Quick, quick, don't make the punters angry. She was a black girl, and she seemed vaguely familiar to Duffy. She was thinnish like the first girl, with a hard-looking, impassive face. She danced a lot better than her predecessor, and was a lot more athletic. She was also a lot dirtier. She played with tits and pubes while she danced, as the other girl had done. But she also leaned right over, stuck her bum in the air, and pulled her cheeks apart so that you could see her cunt and her bum-hole. Then she would bounce over towards a letter box and put her leg right up in the air, resting her foot against the wall of the booth while she dabbled at her cunt with her fingers. After a few seconds she would dance away again, then attract in turn the attention of all the punters with their visors raised and appear to pick out one of them. The lucky man, provided his 50p didn't run out, then had his window squeegeed by the girl's cunt. This happened to Duffy after he had spent about £1.30. It wasn't exactly a turn-on (though it certainly wasn't a turn-off), but it was a bit odd: rather like sitting in your car at a garage while they chammy your windscreen.

Duffy wasn't quite sure why he dropped the fourth 50p into the slot – after all, he knew he'd seen the best part of the show. With other men the action would have sprung from the generosity of the satisfied punter who's been ripped off so many times that he likes to show his appreciation for once. With Duffy it sprang from a still lurking curiosity. He somehow felt he'd seen the black girl before. On his final 50p, he didn't watch her tits or her cunt; he watched her face. There was something familiar about it. Then he switched his gaze and saw it – a thin white scar on the right shoulder. It was the girl who'd been stabbed four years ago, the girl he'd visited in hospital and leaned on a bit.

Duffy waited around outside the Peep Show for a while. He couldn't do too much of this, he realised. Standing around on street corners in Soho was all right as far as the public went: they just thought you were a pimp. But the other pimps and the blues tended to come by for a closer squint at you. After a bit Duffy looked around for a café and saw one forty yards down the street. Not the best location, but he might be able to get a clear view from there. He sat over a coffee – the boredom of it brought back to him his days with the force – and waited for about half an hour. Then the black girl came out of the Peep Show and started walking down the street in his direction. He abandoned his coffee and stepped outside. She was twenty yards short of the café when she suddenly jumped into a taxi and disappeared.

Duffy went home thinking that there were parts of his job he quite enjoyed. What he really needed to discover was how the new power structure of the Golden Mile worked: who owned what, who dealt in what, who fixed and ran what. He could ask Carol, of course; though he didn't like to involve her, especially if the case was going to get anywhere near Sullivan. He could try chasing down a few old contacts; he could see if the black girl – what was she called? – would help. Not that he'd been very nice to her apart from taking her some flowers at the hospital when she'd cut her bum on the baked bean tin. There was another possibility – calling on Renée, that is, if she was still working. Renée was a whore he'd always got on well with, a sharp, businesslike whore with a sense of humour; she'd been around the streets for about twenty years now, and must be pushing forty. But she knew most things that were going on, and was willing to sell most of the things that she knew. If McKechnie wanted an invoice, though, he'd have to whistle for it. Renée didn't exactly fill out V.A.T. forms.

Next morning McKechnie called.

'It's gone up,' was the first thing he said.

Duffy was not surprised. 'How much?'

'Hundred and fifty. But I've got four days to pay. Salvatore said he was feeling generous.'

'That's standard,' said Duffy. 'Did you record it all right?'

'Yes.'

'Then this is what I want you to do. Turn the tape over and start on side two. Phone Sullivan and record your conversation. Take a tough line with him, say you've already lost three hundred and fifty quid thanks to him, tell him the fee's gone up again and you want some action this time. Tell him that when you make the drop you want to be certain that there's an officer watching. Tell him you want a description of that officer and his name and where he'll be, so that you can check that Sullivan is doing what he says he is. Try not to put his back up too much, but pull an outraged-citizen act . . . '

'I *am* outraged,' said McKechnie.

'Of course; sorry. But act like someone who is getting towards the end of his tether and might do something Sullivan wouldn't like. Give the impression you might go to his superiors or to the newspapers or something. I'm sure he'll be hell-bent on calming you down. Do you think you can manage that?'

McKechnie said he thought so.

'When you've made the call, take the tape out, put it in an envelope and give it to your secretary. Tell her' (Duffy quickly thought up some gumshoe ploy which would make McKechnie feel he was getting his money's worth) 'to go to the snack bar at the west end of Paddington Station at three o'clock. I'll be sitting with my back to the counter with a large brown parcel on the seat next to me. She's to ask if the seat is free and when I say it is she's to slip the envelope on to the counter between us. Do you think she can do that?'

'She's proved more or less capable in all I've given her to do so far.'

'Good. Oh, and there's another thing. I'll need some cash for some information. I'm going to talk to a whore, and as you probably know, whores don't give receipts.'

'How much?'

'Not sure. Maybe fifty or so.'

'Mr Duffy, I wouldn't want to find you proving as big a drain on my resources as Mr Salvatore is. Do you follow me?'

'All right. So can you put the fifty in with the tape.'

'No. Take it out of your advance. She may not talk, after all.' That was true enough.

'O.K. And remind me what your secretary's called.'

'Belinda.'

At three o'clock Duffy was at Paddington Station, his back turned to the snack bar counter. Suddenly there was a tap on his shoulder, and a high-pitched voice trilled,

'Oh, Mr Duffy.'

He spun round. It was the secretary. He winced.

'Mr McKechnie asked me to give you this.' She handed him a brown envelope. 'I don't like to be nosy, but I think it's got a tape recording in it.' Then she leaned over to

71

him, smiled, and whispered, 'I say, Mr Duffy, isn't all this *exciting*?'

If Duffy had had them with him, he would have walked out of the snack bar wearing his King Kong mask and his clown's hat, just to make sure that nobody noticed him.

Back at the flat, he found that the first side of the tape didn't have anything unexpected on it. Duffy played it through, mainly just listening to Salvatore's voice. It didn't seem as foreign as McKechnie had described, but it had the authentic tang of a man who's calling all the shots and enjoying it. Towards the end of the conversation, McKechnie said,

'You're squeezing me too hard, don't you know that?'

'Squeezing you, Mr McKechnie? *Squeezing* you? I can promise you that you'd be feeling it if I were. No, no. You're just helping me out with my little cash-flow crisis, that's what you're doing.'

'Where am I going to find a hundred and fifty in four days?'

A little chuckle from the other end of the phone.

'Oh, I'm sure the shareholders will accept a reduced dividend just for this one year.'

'You mean you're going to lay off me?' He sounded whingeingly hopeful.

'No, I don't exactly mean *that*, Mr McKechnie. Indeed, I can't see my cash-flow crisis being solved in the immediate future. I might even have to call on you for some increased sums.'

'I can't find the amount you're asking for.'

'Well, Mr McKechnie, all I can say to that is that you might find yourself called upon to liquefy some of your capital assets.'

'What do you mean?'

'Well, I'm sure you don't need all that storage space you've got. *Two* warehouses – I would have thought with a better storekeeping policy you could probably manage with just the one. Wouldn't you?'

'I couldn't get rid of one of my warehouses.' There was almost a note of panic in McKechnie's voice. 'I couldn't.'

'Suck it and see, Mr McKechnie. Suck it and see.'

On the second side of the tape McKechnie was displaying a lot more bottle. Maybe he'd caught it from Salvatore; maybe he suddenly realised that Duffy would be listening and wanted to put on a less craven performance. After hearing it straight through, Duffy rewound and picked it up again in the middle.

'. . . the last time.'

'Well, we'll do our best, McKechnie, I won't promise you anything more than that.'

'I haven't been too impressed with your best so far, Sullivan. I'm just suggesting to you that now might be the time to get your finger out. I'm suggesting that what I want this time is some assurance.'

'Like what?'

'I want to know that one of your men is at the scene when I make my drop.'

'O.K., you have my assurance.'

'I want more than that, Sullivan. I want to know who's going to be there; I want a description of him so that I can check he's there; I want his name and rank so that if necessary I can get in touch with him later.'

'You trying to teach me how to run my department, McKechnie? I'm not having some . . . . coming on to my patch and telling me how to run my shop. I'm not having you interfering with my boys.'

'I hope you won't be too unco-operative, Sullivan.'

'What do you mean?'

'Just what I say.' McKechnie played it cool. 'I think it would be in everyone's best interests if the police afforded a local trader the normal degree of co-operation.'

'Hmmm.' If Duffy had been Sullivan, he would have

called McKechnie's bluff and told him to bugger off. Sullivan was more cautious. 'Well, I'll see what I can do. I'm not telling you any officer's name or rank, but I'll give you a description of one of the officers covering the drop. Ring me when you know where it's going to be.'

Duffy stopped the tape. Then he ran it back for a few seconds and got Sullivan speaking: ' . . . run my department, McKechnie? I'm not having some . . . . coming on to my patch and telling me how to run my shop.' There was a gap in the tape about two and a half seconds long. Duffy rang McKechnie.

'There's a gap in the tape.'

'What?'

'There's a gap in the tape. What was Sullivan saying?'

'Oh, that, Mr Duffy, yes there is, you're quite right. It's quite all right, it wasn't anything of relevance to the case.'

'What was it and why did you wipe it?'

'Well . . . you see, it struck me that if this tape ever . . . well, ever became part of an investigation for instance, if it ever became part of a case, you know what I mean, Mr Duffy?'

'All right.'

'Then I wouldn't want to be thought of by those listening to the case in the terms in which the Superintendent chose to describe me. You may think I'm being over-sensitive, but that's how I reacted anyway.'

'And what did he call you?'

'I'd need your assurance that you wouldn't repeat it.'

'All right.'

'Well, he called me . . . a syphilitic sheep-fucker.'

Duffy smiled into the telephone.

'Your secret is safe with me, Mr McKechnie.'

This was on a Tuesday. The drop was on the Friday. At eleven McKechnie phoned Duffy at his flat.

'Same time. One o'clock. Dustbins again. Brewer Street. Dustbins by the garage entrance next to Gino's

Delicatessen. The one farthest away from the shop. Sullivan said he'd have a man in the window of the café opposite Gino's. Said I should come down Brewer Street on the wrong side, pretending not to see Gino's, check that his man was there, and then cross the road and make the drop.'

'What did he say his man looked like?'

'He said he'd be wearing a scarlet tie so that I'd see him easily through the window. He wouldn't tell me anything more about what he looked like.'

'O.K. You do exactly as both of them told you. I'll be in touch later.'

Duffy wanted to be in place early, to see Sullivan's man arrive. But Sullivan's man would have to get there early to make sure he got a window seat in a café at one o'clock. So Duffy would have to be there even earlier. He took a cab. McKechnie would have to pay for this necessary luxury.

He got to Brewer Street around eleven thirty and walked slowly down its length in punter style. He spotted Gino's quickly, and then the café on the other side of the road. The dustbins could be seen easily from the café. But the trouble was, there wasn't anywhere obvious for Duffy to place himself and be able to observe both the drop and the café. There was a pub fifteen yards down from the café: he could see the drop from there, but then he wouldn't be able to see Sullivan's man. Or there was a dirty bookshop from where he could see the café but not the drop; perhaps he could buy something, so that he wouldn't get thrown out, and then just browse for a bit. No, that was no good; he had to see the drop. Then why not sit in the café as well? It might get a bit awkward when both he and Sullivan's man got up to tail the pick-up at exactly the same time, but he'd just have to cross that bridge when he came to it.

Duffy decided on the café. He went in at about twelve and sat at a side table away from the window. He ordered a meal he didn't in the least need, and began his wait. Twelve fifteen and a few early lunchers arrived. Twelve thirty and the place was really starting to fill up. There were only two free tables left in the window. Twelve forty-five and there was only one. At least the other customers would give Duffy cover, but where was Sullivan's man? Then he noticed that the one free table had a plastic Reserved sign on it. That was getting a bit lordly. Twelve fifty and the man in the scarlet tie sauntered in. Duffy took a quick look and put his head down.

Shaw. Christ, he hadn't reckoned for that. Old Rick Shaw, as he'd been nicknamed at West Central. He hadn't allowed for that; he'd thought it would be some wet-ear he'd never set eyes on before. That changed everything. He didn't at all fancy trying to tail the pick-up man and stay out of Shaw's way at the same time.

At twelve fifty-five Duffy carefully left the café, turning his head away as he walked past the window occupied by Shaw. He got to the pub and saw to his relief that there was a knot of drinkers on the pavement. With a half of bitter in his hand he stood around as if he could almost be part of their group. At twelve fifty-nine McKechnie went past the pub, walking as if looking out for something, peering rather shortsightedly into shops. He was doing it well, Duffy thought. He saw him reach the café, go past it for ten yards, stop, turn, then suddenly pretend to spot Gino's on the other side of the road. At a minute past one he reached the dustbin and made the drop. Then he headed off back the way he'd come, turned down Great Windmill Street and disappeared.

At four minutes past one Shaw came out of the café, turned sharp right, didn't give the dustbin a glance, and hurried off. That was not part of the plan at all, as far as Duffy had imagined it. Was Shaw merely there to keep McKechnie happy, and was Sullivan in effect simply handing the money over to Salvatore? Or was Shaw just

76

part of a two-man team, and Sullivan had wisely pulled him out in case someone watching had seen McKechnie look in at the restaurant window? Still, at least it meant that Duffy wouldn't have to worry about mixing his tail with Shaw's.

At one fifteen a scruffy youth in denims came hurrying down the street. He stopped by the dustbins, rooted about in the right-hand one, then the middle one, finally landed on the one where the envelope was, picked it out and stuffed it in his pocket. Whether he'd gone through all three dustbins because he wanted to look like an authentic rag-picker or whether he'd done so because he was all fucked up and couldn't remember which bin to look in, Duffy didn't know or care.

Duffy had guessed that the youth would head east along Brewer Street. This wasn't a difficult gamble, as west would take him out into Regent Street, and he didn't see this kid losing a tail by mingling indistinguishably with the clientèle in Jaeger's. As the scruff was making up the hundred yards to get level with him, Duffy squinted round looking for likely police tails. Part of being taught how to tail is being taught how to recognise tails and lose them. The kid was almost level with him and nothing likely had presented itself. He let the kid go thirty, forty yards before deciding he couldn't let him get any farther away; not in Soho. He'd just have to risk it about Sullivan's tail.

Duffy closed down the gap quickly: you could lose someone in ten yards at that end of Brewer Street. Shit, he was cutting through to Berwick Street market. Duffy should have predicted that. Past the Revuebar, and then in among the stalls. One person pushing a bit in a street market didn't show. Another person pushing to keep up with the first person showed a lot. The youth dodged about a bit among the stalls. Fortunately he wasn't very competent; or maybe he hadn't been trained very well, or maybe he thought he didn't need to try. After a bit of hide-and-seek he dodged down St Anne's Court, into Dean Street, across Bateman, and into Frith. Duffy turned the corner into Frith in time to see him disappearing up the steps of the Double Blue Cinema Club.

Duffy paused. He was sure of two things. One was that Sullivan hadn't had the kid tailed: Shaw had simply walked off and that had been the end of the surveillance. The other was that if he rushed up the steps into the cinema straight away he might as well be wearing a tin badge and whistling the theme from *High Noon*. He stood around for a bit, waited for a couple of punters to go into the club, prayed for another celluloid lecher to turn up quickly, and when he did, followed him quickly up the steps.

5

The grey-suited punter Duffy followed up the steps of the Double Blue looked round nervously at him, as if Duffy were a private detective hired by his wife. At the plywood box office he bought a subscription for ten pounds and paid a fiver to go in. He disappeared ahead of Duffy.

'Member?' asked the cashier, who looked like a soiled hippy.

'No. But I'll have the normal rates, not the ones you charge shits in suits.' Duffy knew there was no real 'normal' rate; it fluctuated according to the punter, and often the cashier's wages at the end of the day depended on how much he took. It was up to the man in the box office to find out how much the market could bear.

'All right. Fiver for membership, three-fifty to go in.'

Duffy looked at him quizzically. 'Sure it isn't two-fifty?'

'Nah. Never has been, chief. More than my job's worf to drop it that far.'

Duffy nodded. Hell, it was only McKechnie's money.

'Name?' The cashier had pulled out a grubby white membership card on which he had inscribed a number and a date.

'Daniel Drough.' The hippy wrote it out in capitals, clearly finding it a change from the long run of J. Smiths and H. Wilsons that he was used to. Duffy took the card and went into the cinema.

There were two dozen people inside a large corridor of a room, with a screen about ten feet by six at the end of it. While waiting for his eyes to acclimatise, Duffy watched the film. It was like a larger version of the 10p Mini-Movies he'd watched, but a bit dirtier. It also had very bad sound.

There were two girls, supposedly lying on a beach, who had taken their bikinis off and were dabbing palmfuls of sun-oil on each other; it made a slapping noise, like the sea against a harbour wall. Then one of them produced a vibrator from out of nowhere, and switched it on. It sounded as if someone had started to Hoover the beach. She applied this to the other girl's tits; the other girl smiled. Then she applied it to the girl's pubes, whereupon the second girl immediately flung her legs apart as if for gynaecological examination, threw her head back, and began to pant. In order to be heard over the sound of the vibrator she had to pant very loudly. It sounded as if a large sheepdog had been harnessed to a Hoover, was pulling it up and down the beach, and getting very tired. Duffy's cock informed him that this wasn't a very good film.

He looked round the punters, searching for his man. He covered half of them, then moved his seat. Movement isn't very popular in these cinemas. It disturbs the entranced communion between the man in his seat and the image on the screen; it makes the punters shifty and guilty about their hard-ons. Some managements send a patrolling heavy round every so often to make sure the punters aren't jerking off over the seats; others decide this is bad for business as it disturbs the customers, install washable plastic seats, and pay the cleaners a bit extra.

Duffy couldn't see his man among the second half of the audience either. He looked around the cinema, while careful not to catch any punter's eye for fear of enraging him. Down at the end, next to the screen, there was a toilet (the clubs are wisely punctilious about G.L.C. regulations on membership procedures and toilets). The side walls of the cinema were solid. The box office had just been a plywood insert into the front six feet of the building.

Duffy got up again and went to the toilet. A narrow

corridor ran past it for another fifteen feet or so. Duffy went along to the end and saw some stairs doubling back up to the left. At the foot of the stairs on the right was an emergency exit. The two horizontal push-bars, one on each door, had been chained together; the padlock which held them looked rusty. Duffy slowly walked up the stairs, trying not to make any noise. When he was about halfway up he heard a door open, and footsteps at about the level of his head. Immediately he started walking up at a normal pace, whistling quietly as he did so. When he got to the top of the stairs he saw a large, ginger-haired man with glasses closing a door on the right.

'Where's the pisser, mate?' he asked in a no-trouble voice.

'You walked right past it,' the man replied. 'First bloke to walk past our pisser,' he added genially, 'yer nose must be all blocked up.'

Duffy pulled out a handkerchief and blew hard, then sniffed, and acted being knocked out by the stink. 'Think I can find it now, mate,' he said, and headed off downstairs. There'd been three rooms at the top of the stairs, and he could hear voices coming from the one on the right. He walked back to the toilet, waited a few seconds, and pulled the chain; nothing happened; he pulled again and smiled at the wasted subterfuge.

He sat in the cinema for a bit longer while a girl with big tits who ran a sex shop invited customers into her back room for a bit of mild fladge (Duffy caught himself wondering who was minding the shop in the meantime). She pulled up her skirt, took down her knickers and leaned over a desk. The men pretended to beat her with a riding crop while she made a whimpering noise which the sound system turned into the cry of an eviscerated goose.

As Duffy left he had a bantering word with the hippy cashier, who confessed he found the films 'really boring', that he'd 'been through that scene'. Duffy recommended that he try again, and mentioned the sex shop number. 'I mean, maybe tits aren't your scene, but if they are, man, then that's the film for you, I'd say.'

'Nah, I think they're all really boring.'

Meanwhile, Duffy had completed his casual examination of the locks on the cinema doors; he said goodbye and wandered off.

When he got back home he phoned McKechnie.

'What did Sullivan say?'

'He said he couldn't understand it. He'd put two of his best men on the job, and the bloke had got clean away again.'

'Did he say how?'

'Yes, he ran into Regent Street and jumped into a cab. Sullivan's men waited on the pavement but there wasn't another cab for a while.'

'Did you believe him?'

'No. Should I have?'

'No. Did you tell him you didn't?'

'No. What really happened?'

'The red-tie merchant in the café when you made the drop got up and left almost at once, just scarpered. Whether there was another guy or not I can't be sure; but if there was, he couldn't tail a man in a wheelchair. He was nowhere when I got to the end of my run.'

'Where was that.'

'A place called the Double Blue. It's a cinema club in Frith Street. The bloke vanished inside. Somewhere upstairs. I couldn't follow him.'

'So what do we do now?'

'Dunno for the moment. I'll nose around for a bit. By the way, the cinema cost me eight-fifty.'

'Got a receipt?'

'I've got a membership card.'

'I said receipts, Duffy.'

'I'll tell you about the films in incredible detail if you like.'

'It wouldn't be the same.'

'No – it'd probably be better.' McKechnie laughed.

Duffy wasn't sure what line to follow. He sat down to review what had happened so far. Some things were certain, some things were hopelessly ambiguous. Someone had cut McKechnie's wife for a start. Someone was now trying to presh him, though how far was anyone's guess. Someone with a sense of humour was using a dead racketeer's name. Then there was Sullivan – what was he up to? Was he simply taking the easy way out by missing the pick-ups, or was he taking a cut? What was Shaw doing – old Rick? Was he just doing what Sullivan told him, or was he being cut in? He'd always remembered Shaw as a copper who didn't go in for accepting too many Christmas turkeys. Still, every year around the Golden Mile brought different temptations. He knew how it happened: you didn't take the free booze even if everyone else did; you didn't take the first girl you got offered; you turned down the smokes and the snort; and then something quite trivial happened, like you asked for a couple of days to pay at the bookie's. Quite suddenly, the place had got you. It wasn't necessarily that there was a particular gang always on the look-out to bend coppers (though sometimes there was); it was somehow the place that got you. It was one square mile of pressure, and everyone had a weak point.

Duffy felt he had to know some more background. He really needed to talk to someone like Shaw, but that was out of the question. Maybe Carol; or maybe that wasn't fair; well, maybe he could ask her about the place without letting her know what he was up to. Apart from Carol, there was Renée: he ought to go and have a chat with her, if only for old times' sake. That was a dangerous phrase, 'old times' sake' – if he started thinking like that he'd be sentimentalising about Sullivan before he knew where he was. And then there was the black girl at the Peep Show. What was she called? Something with a B or a P. Belinda? No, that was McKechnie's dumb secretary. That was it – Polly. Not that she owed him any favours.

And then there were a few other things which Duffy wondered about. One was that McKechnie didn't seem as worried by everything as Duffy thought he ought to be; he even seemed to find parts of it almost exciting. No, maybe he was just phlegmatic; and he had seemed genuinely upset when he'd told Duffy about what had happened to his wife. Perhaps McKechnie was really much richer than he thought, and could soak up a lot more presh; though you'd never guess, to look at the shack he operated from. It wasn't exactly buzzing with clients, either. Still, maybe that sort of business was mainly mail order. But then – there were so many buts in the case – what about the gap on the tape? McKechnie had been completely plausible about it; but was it Sullivan's style to call a member of the public a 'syphilitic sheep-fucker'? Well, that again was possible; actually, quite probable. And finally there was the little incident at Paddington Station that nagged at Duffy: if the secretary had managed to remember about getting there, arriving at the right time and the right place, and recognising him, could she be so thick that she didn't carry out the rest of the instructions he had given McKechnie? Or what if McKechnie had changed those instructions, what if she'd actually been doing exactly as she'd been told? That was an undermining thought; but Duffy decided to shrug it off. McKechnie probably wasn't an entirely straight-up-and-down guy, but which of his clients ever had been? And did you expect a guy who sold King Kong masks in Soho to behave like a clergyman? There was one rule you tried to stick to in this business: you believed the client was dealing straight with you until you had strong evidence to the contrary.

He rang Carol and asked her if she'd like to come round that evening. She said she couldn't, she was going to the pictures (who with? But the rules said you weren't allowed to ask). She could come the next night, though. Duffy said Yes please, and he'd make her the best toasted cheese she'd had since the last time she'd had toasted cheese.

He contemplated another evening alone in his flat. Maybe he'd better go out and find someone. Soho made you randy, there was no doubt about that. Not the films he'd seen – the Hoover, the sheepdog and the goose – or the memory of having his windscreen squeegeed in the Peep Show; it was just being there. The air over mill towns used to be heavy with a precipitate of soot; you breathed it into your lungs and body; over Soho, the air seemed filled with a precipitate of sex.

Duffy's mind idled over the choice between trawling for a man and trawling for a woman. To Duffy it was like choosing between bacon and egg and bacon and tomato. Whichever you decided on you had a good time; it was just what your taste-buds felt like that evening. Women were usually less likely to leave you needing a visit to the clinic. On the other hand they were a bit more expensive; they tended not to stand their round if they were going to go to bed with you later; and some of them made the sentimental mistake of believing that because Duffy was nice to them it meant that he wanted to see them again. Then he had to be firm, and tell them no, and that often added a sour note to breakfast.

The other thing was that, in practical terms, men could be more relied upon if you wanted to get laid. You spent longer chatting up women than you did men; and even if you were in a singles bar where it was generally assumed that everyone was on the prowl, it was still part of the accepted convention that a girl had every right to dump you with a final No, even if all evening she'd been giving off signals which said Yes. Whereas if you went to a gay club, you never left disappointed. Not everyone went there determined to get laid, of course; there was a certain amount of 'Well, I'll see', and 'Try me later'; but as long as you were clean and neat, you were bound to end up with someone. There was rarely any of that breakfast trouble, either. Indeed, what some of the guys you brought back wanted to do was just get up and leave before the sheets were dry. Well, that was O.K. by Duffy too.

It looked as if it was heading for another evening down at the Alligator. Besides, if he were seeing Carol tomorrow, it always gave him a jolt if he'd spent the previous night with a girl. And that spoiled the previous night as well; it had him making all sorts of comparisons which weren't a good idea. No, Duffy decided, it would definitely have to be a guy tonight. He headed off to the bathroom to smarten himself up.

A few hours later, he finished his evening at the Alligator with Jack, a gentle, blond American from the Mid-West who was hitch-hiking round Europe with a copy of the *Spartacus Gay Guide to Europe* and a reverent determination to visit every major club and bar listed in it. The tourism side of the venture almost outweighed the gayness side of it: Jack had been sipping a Campari at the Alligator in the manner of a camera-laden tripper lighting a candle at Chartres. He almost had to be reminded about wanting to get laid. Over breakfast, Jack confessed a shy desire to start up his own *Good Gay Guide* along the lines of the *Good Food Guide*, relying on reports from members and occasionally sending out inspectors to make spot checks on establishments which seemed to be slipping. Duffy said he'd get in touch if ever he needed a job.

After Jack had left, Duffy tidied up, changed the sheets for when Carol came (and for if Carol stayed, which weren't at all the same thing) and went off to track down

Renée. She'd always operated from a little flat in an alley off Wardour Street; it was a two-girl gaff, partly for mutual protection and partly in case clients wanted a sandwich job or an exhibition. She'd always worked for the same pimp, called Ronnie, who owned the flat, gave her what protection she needed, and took the usual cut. Renée was a lot smarter than Ronnie, though, and after she hit thirty she persuaded him to adopt a system whereby each year – as she got older and the competition got tougher and her earning potential got a bit less – she would pay him a slightly smaller percentage of what she earned. She pointed out what a good name this would get Ronnie among the other whores, and how this would make it easier for him to get new girls.

Ronnie had bought the scheme, perhaps imagining that Renée would give up at thirty-three or so. But she'd soldiered on, and, as she had planned, the scheme had worked to her advantage. Ronnie had moaned a bit, but kept to his promise after Renée had threatened to bad-mouth him all the way from Soho Square to Piccadilly Circus. That had brought him to heel; and then, to keep him sweet, Renée had upped the rent of the girls she shared the flat with.

As Duffy turned into Wardour Street, he remembered his visits to Renée. Money had occasionally changed hands, though strictly for information received. She had from time to time offered him a Christmas box (she'd smiled as she pronounced the phrase), but he'd thought it best to refuse. Still, he carried on calling on her, often just for chats; and he always followed the cardinal rule of scarpering when a client arrived.

Duffy saw the two lighted bell-pushes labelled RENÉE and SUZIE, pressed the top one, and walked up. He remembered the landing: one door straight ahead, with a card on the outside saying SUZIE; the other, to the right, saying RENÉE. It looked as if the gaff was two separate flats, but in fact they connected up and had an alarm system from one to the other. You knocked on the door and either it opened or you got a shout of 'Five minutes, love', like an A.S.M. giving an actor his call.

Duffy knocked on the door on the right. It opened, and there was Renée in a long dressing gown, her dark hair half piled up on top of her head and half tumbling down one side in long curls to make an elaborately confected coiffure. She looked a bit older, a bit plumper, as she briefly cast an eye over him in the way that whores do, to see if he was either copper or someone from the whores' blacklist; it was a dispassionate gaze, like that of a shop manager checking a credit card.

'Come in, love,' she said, and backed into the room. As she did so she let the dressing gown fall back so that he could see a black garter belt and stockings and a black bra.

'Nothing dirty,' she announced, before he had time to close the door. 'I don't do nothing dirty. I don't do it up the bum and I keep me mouth to meself. It's ten if you want it straight, eight for the hands, an extra two if you want to see me tits; and there're a few other things I might do but you've gotta ask for them.'

'Renée,' he said, 'I'm Duffy.'

'Sorry, love, never remember a face in my business.'

'No, I'm Duffy, I'm not a client . . .'

Renée looked up, very cross.

'What d'yer mean, you're not a fucking client? Whatcher doing here if yer not a client?' She looked at him again, then suddenly she recognised him.

'Duffy. Of course. Duffy.' She looked embarrassed. 'Why didn't you stop me in the sales spiel, you bastard?'

'Didn't have time. You never let a fellow get in edgeways, Renée, did you?'

'I'd let him in edgeways; just wouldn't let him in from the back. Hey, Duffy, what've you come to see me for?' She pulled her dressing gown across her body. 'And I let you see what's become of me. I oughta charge you for that, Duffy. What've you come to see me for?'

'Well . . .'

'Oh, Christ, I've just remembered. I've just remembered why you stopped coming to see me. I didn't know you were bent, Duffy. I mean, I don't judge, but I didn't know you were bent. Bent and little boys, it was, wasn't it, Duffy, that's what they said. I don't judge, but little boys I don't approve of, I'd better tell you that straight out.'

'It wasn't little boys.' Duffy was furious. Is that what the whisper was? 'Who said it was little boys?'

'Oh, you know, that's what they said. People. You don't remember who.'

'It was a fit-up, Renée. I was fitted up by someone to have me thrown out. The kid said he was nineteen when the coppers kicked the door in, but he could have been twenty-five. I thought he was, but he told the blues he was nineteen. It was a fit-up, Renée.'

'Sorry to hear it, Duffy.' Renée was sceptical about coppers who were flung out of the force; they always said they'd been fitted up. Still, Duffy had always seemed to be fairly honest.

'Is that why you never took Renée's Christmas box, Duffy? 'Cos you were bent?'

'I was only a bit bent, Renée. I like fish as well as meat. It's no problem to me. But it wasn't little boys; it's *never* been little boys.' Duffy was still cross. Who did he have to thank for that: fucking Sullivan? Another of his little avuncular acts?

'O.K., Duffy, calm down.'

'And I didn't take the Christmas box because, well, for one thing I knew you were much too smart not to find a use for it later. I knew that I'd be after someone, or a mate of mine might be, and then there'd be a phone call from our Renée and she'd say, "Duffy, remember that Christmas box? Well, now I've got a little something to ask you in return." I knew you were much too sharp not to use that sooner or later.'

'You're no fool, Duffy.'

Duffy nodded agreement; with someone like Renée you always had to work out exactly where you stood.

'Now, what have you come back for if it's not to add to poor old Renée's pension fund?'

'Well, I might be able to make a contribution. It's information I need, Renée.'

'Not back in the force, are you?'

'No. I'm – well, let's say I'm acting in a freelance capacity for a certain party who's being preshed locally.'

'What's wrong with the wonderful boys in blue?'

'Well, it looks as if all their blind eyes are pointing in the same direction at the moment if you can imagine.'

'I might have heard of it happening before. And so this particular fellow called for Duffy?'

'All right.'

'Why you?'

'I'd been recommended.'

That was another thing which Duffy was puzzling over: who'd recommended him to McKechnie. What had he said? 'I asked around'? Where had he asked, Duffy wondered. Certainly nowhere near his last two jobs – advising on a burglar-alarm system for a factory in Hounslow, and telling a slice of posh trash where to hide her jewels. (She'd been too mean to insure them or buy a safe and too lazy to put them in the bank and take them out when she needed them: she just wanted Duffy to go round the house with her and tell her the last place a thief would think of looking. She'd been reading some story, she said, where something had been cleverly hidden in the most obvious place and no one had ever found it: wasn't that *such* a good idea? Duffy told her that the most obvious place for her jewels was in her jewel box, and what chance did she think there was of burglars looking

90

there? She'd looked a bit put down, and Duffy went on to rubbish the whole theory of keeping things in obvious places: lots of burglars are so thick they only look in obvious places. So what about somewhere that isn't *terribly* obvious and isn't *terribly* difficult, she asked? Then the medium-grade burglars find your jewels, Duffy said. So they settled for the hardest place after all. Then it turned out that what she'd *actually* been thinking about was the elephant's-foot waste-paper basket that grandpa had brought back from India and which had a false bottom. Duffy said that this was ideal, wrote out a bill for fifty pounds, tore it up, wrote out a new one for fifty guineas, sent it off and swore to himself that if the posh trash didn't pay he'd make sure a little leak went in the right direction. To someone, for instance, who collected waste-paper baskets.)

'But the Mile's changed a bit, I expect, since I was here. I thought you might be able to fill me in. You know, who runs what, who's new, what sort of presh is on, that sort of thing.'

'Funny you should ask me that, Duffy, I was only talking to Ronnie about it the other day. I'm not a moaner, you know that, and it's not just an old tart talking who's getting elbowed off the street by young scrubbers . . .'

'You're looking younger than ever,' Duffy responded automatically.

'Don't shit me, Duffy, I know I'm getting to a difficult age for a tart. You get past a certain age and you've got a choice: either you're content with your regulars – and I am on the whole, I've got a nice bunch, quite clean most of 'em – though you gradually see them dropping off a bit; you know, trying someone a bit younger or a black tart, or someone who does something different. Or you do . . . oh, what's the word for it, Duffy, you do that thing what big companies are always doing . . .'

'Diversify?'

'That's right. You have to diversify. And that, believe you me, is a U-fer-mism. Diversify means you have to take anyone who comes up those stairs, diversify means taking mean shits who want to hurt you. It means you have to let punters fuck you up the bum, and I'm *never* going to do that. It means you have to let them give you a bashing with whips and stuff. Some of them . . . well, I'm not easily shocked, you know that, Duffy, some of them, soon as they see I'm not fifteen, they want to do things I won't even tell Suzie next door, corrupt her poor mind. Personally, I blame all this pornography the Labour Government let in, that's what I blame.'

Duffy smiled, though he wasn't sure if he was meant to; Renée often laughed when she was serious. But one thing was clear: she wouldn't be diversifying.

'When I started in this gaff it was a nice trade, being on the streets. Sure, there were a few nasties now and then, but it was a nice, friendly trade. You set yourself up, you built up your custom, you got known for what you did best, and you turned an honest penny. You saw some things which you probably shouldn't have seen, but you kept your trap shut. I remember when I used to have a cabinet minister from Harold Macmillan's Government in here regular as clockwork; every Friday after adjournment, before he caught the train back to his constituency. Well, he was only a junior minister actually, but I wouldn't tell anyone his name. That's what the business was all about. And I wouldn't tell *you* his name, neither.' Renée looked at him belligerently.

'I'm not asking.'

'That was nearly twenty years ago, anyway. I liked the work then. You had nice holidays, the streets were friendlier, almost everyone asked for it straight, and if they didn't they were very apologetic about it. You'd say, "Come on love, out with it, you can't shock Renée," and then they'd babble on about boots or whips or school uniforms or something and you'd say, "Sorry, love, I'd really like to, I just don't have the equipment with me, but I tell you who you ought to see and that's Annie," and they look terribly grateful and go off and you quickly ring up Annie and tell her you've sent someone round and she either does the same back or sends you a few quid for the introduction.

'We weren't cut-throats because we knew there was enough punter to go round. But that's changed a lot since then. You've no idea the way the average tart's living's been attacked in the last twenty years, Duffy, no idea. There was that Permissiveness for a start, when all the girls who didn't use to suddenly started putting out. *That* didn't do us any good, as you can imagine. And then there was that Women's Liberation which amounted to exactly the same thing. Then all the films started getting dirtier and dirtier, and the books did too. You could go to the theatre and see girls waggling their twats on stage and everyone was calling it art so that they didn't have to put a newspaper over their head when they came out. Art – fart, if you ask me.' Renée was really getting launched. Duffy just sat back and listened.

'So what happened to us was that a bit of good old-fashioned straight with tarts got the squeeze. Sure, there's enough of it to keep you going still, but when fellows could get it at home or from their secretaries or from any old pub scrubber for nothing, why should they lay out good money on us? So two things happened. One was that we started noticing we were getting a bigger percentage of oddballs than before – you know, crips and hunchies and things. Not that I really mind them, they're quite sweet really; it's just that, you know, given the choice . . .

'And the second thing was that the punters weren't wanting so much straight as before. All of a sudden lots of punters wanted you to wank them off. I mean, you'd think

93

that was the one thing they could do for themselves, wouldn't you? I don't mind doing it, as long as you've got something to catch the drips, but I do find it's hard on the wrists. I mean, five or six punters in a row and none of them want to put it in, it takes it out of you. You feel you've been lifting boxes of apples all day. I *did* think of charging more for that than for straight, I don't mind telling you.

'And it wasn't just wanking. Suddenly, they were all wanting mouth stuff. Well, I don't do that, I really don't, I think it's disgusting really. But I always make sure the girl I share with will do it, then they can pop across the landing if they really want that. The other things, too, well, as I say, I blame all that Labour pornography. And all those film clubs and massage parlours – have you seen them, Duffy?'

Duffy nodded.

'They've been a terrible blow, too. All the punters just go and sit in the dark and watch films of people fucking. What good is that to trade? And as for the parlours, you know I sometimes wonder why they haven't run us girls out of business. I suppose the only thing that keeps people coming to us is the thought that they might go into a parlour and find out they had to have a real massage – have some great fat German woman hitting them in the back like she was beating steak, and then push them in an ice-cold plunge shower, and all for fifteen nicker or something.'

Renée laughed. She liked the idea of it. She didn't take her business too seriously, even when she was complaining about it. Duffy laughed as well.

'Still, I suppose that isn't quite what you wanted to ask me.'

'Not quite. I was thinking a bit more about who runs what, and that sort of thing.'

'Well, that's changed a lot too, and if you ask me it's not

got any nicer neither. And it all happens so quickly you can't keep up with it. Now, the old days, it was all the Maltese boys. They got a really bad press, the Malties did, but I always thought that was, you know, racial prejudice. They'd stick a knife in you soon as look at you if they thought you were shitting them, but I never had no trouble. They used to buy up houses and set them up real regular. Strip club in the basement, dirty bookshop on the ground floor, escort agency on the middle floor, tarts on the top. It was like a layer cake, that's what it was like. And the runner would come round every Friday evening and collect a tenner from every floor. Forty quid the building. Sounds peanuts now, doesn't it? But I suppose the rates were much cheaper then, and these Maltese boys, you know, they had a sense of what they wanted out of their investments, and if they got forty quid a house, they were happy. Mind you, you had to pay, even if business was bad, otherwise you'd be sitting at home and suddenly a paraffin heater might come flying through the window. Not nice, they weren't, when they were riled, the Malties; but they were fair, I'll say that.

'Then there was a big clean-up and lots of the Malties got put in pris or kicked out; some of them just ran away and got given a stretch in their absence. And I suppose everyone thought, Oh well, that's cleaned out the Malties, now we'll be able to take the children walking up and down Old Compton Street with ice cream cones in their mitts. Silly buggers. What they should have known was that the Malties were the best we've ever had. Just because they put the Malties in pris, it doesn't mean the tarts are going to go away, does it? Stands to reason. It just means someone new's going to come in and take their slice.

'Well, that's what happened of course. You know that as well as I do, Duffy. Ever since, there's been absolutely no stability. No stability at all. A few local pimps got bigger, some fellows from up north muscled in; we've had a few Paddies, only they didn't last long; there's the blacks there now, and even some of the Chinkies have tried expanding a bit. I mean, it stands to reason, doesn't it? And then, after the Malties went, all your wonderful boys in blue started getting bent as hairpins. With the Malties, it was just a little bit here, a little bit there, either side step over the mark and they go down for a bit. But when the Malties went, didn't the blues get grabby? The tarts were paying the pimps, the pimps were paying the blues, the tarts were paying the blues. It was a real free-for-all, I can tell you, and the coppers were getting way over the top.

'Then the coppers got sorted out, or rather they didn't really get sorted out, just packed off for an early retirement and all their winnings stacked safely away in their wives' names. It's disgusting, it really is. Coppers' cows sitting on all that money.'

'Who took over from Salvatore?' Duffy thought it was time to be specific.

Renée looked quite nostalgic.

'Dear old Emilio. I had him, you know. Only once or twice, but I had him. He had a funny habit. After he'd finished, he'd get dressed, wouldn't say a word, put on his hat, went to the door, raised his hat, and went off. Not a word, and no money. I mean, the first time it happened I told him the price before, and when he didn't put it straight in the dish I assumed he'd give it me later. But he didn't. Just walked off. Then a couple of days later your money arrives in the post. Always happened that way. I suppose he liked to think he was the big boss getting everything for free at the time. But he never didn't pay.'

'And when he died?'

'I think he had a nephew or something, but he wasn't up to much and got chased out. The Chinkies took a bit, took the smokes and whatnot. The restaurants and things went to Big Eddy, I'm fairly sure of that. The whores went to a black guy, name of O'Reilly.'

'Who runs smokes and the rest?'

'Chinkies. Old Max a bit, but not very seriously. Mad Keith. Finlay.'

'Whores?'

'Big Eddy. O'Reilly. Mad Keith. There's a batch of bents – pardon – run by Fat Eric. Remember him?'

'The one who used to boast about how hairy he was – "From the tip of my nose to the tip of my dick" – that Eric?'

'Yes. And Henderson. He's quite big in tarts at the moment.'

'What about the bookshops and the clubs?'

'Same as the whores, mainly. Mad Keith owns the Peep Shows. And I think there's a new bloke called Johnny Grease who's got a few.'

'Protection?'

'Well, bit of everyone, as you know. Depends who's biggest in any particular area, doesn't it?'

'Who's big round Rupert Street?'

'Which end? South or north of the Avenue? It makes a difference.'

'South.'

'Ah, pity. North, I'd definitely have said Big Eddy. But south, well, it's a fairly quiet patch, usually. Maybe O'Reilly. He's the black guy.'

'Hmm. What about the coppers?'

Renée looked at him sharply.

'You sure you're not with them?'

'Cross my heart.'

'You're not one of them clean-up coppers are you? A copper for coppers?'

'I wish I was.'

'Say me no.'

'No.'

'Good. Now tell me how much you're paying me for what I'm telling you.'

'Twenty-five . . . ?'

Renée laughed.

'Ha, Duffy, it's all coming back to me now. You never were any good at that sort of haggling, were you? Now, let me remember. You're offering twenty-five. That means you've got fifty to spend, so I'll ask for seventy-five and then in a few minutes we'll fix on sixty and you'll be wondering if you'll have to find the extra ten out of your own pocket.'

Duffy grinned.

'Sixty it is, and probably ten from me. What about the coppers?'

'Problems with the coppers. They're in a very jumpy mood at the moment. Ronnie and me were talking about it the other day. They're being very unpredictable. Some of the time they let everything go, you'd almost think they weren't there. And then again they might jump on you with everything because one of your seams isn't straight. It's almost as if they don't know who's running them themselves.'

'Anyone particularly bent at the moment?'

'Hard to say. One or two of the younger ones go visiting a tart or two, but that's standard. From what I know, it's no worse than usual. It's just that, well, the coppers are giving off a very nasty smell at the moment.'

'Anyone in particular? Stanton? Wetherby? Sullivan? Shaw?'

'Stanton's left. Didn't you know?'

'No. The others?'

'Nothing I can lay my finger on. Maybe they're just a bit jumpy about things. Something's going on somewhere, I'm sure.'

'Do you know who's moving, Renée? Who's on the grab? Who's upsetting all your stability?'

'You know what happens to tarts that talk?'

Duffy nodded. He'd had to identify a couple of them in his time – on the slab.

'I'm not gabby, you see. I'm just a tart that speaks her mind, everyone knows that. But I'm not a tart that squeals to coppers. Never have been.' It wasn't true, but she had her own picture of herself to protect.

'I understand, Renée, and I'm not a copper. I'm not in the force. I've never been near West Central for four years. I'm just an old friend come to call.'

Renée looked at him, raised an eyebrow, and continued.

'Well, it's got to be Big Eddy. And it's not because he tried to put the squeeze on Ronnie the other day. Rang up about how the books in one of Ronnie's shops might go up if someone threw a firelighter through the door. But he's on the move, no doubt about that. It's bad news when someone gets as hungry as Big Eddy.'

'Big Eddy who?'

'Martoff. Big Eddy Martoff. His dad was one of the Malties that got rounded up. Married a nice tart, the dad did. Sad thing was, he died in pris. Eddy was a teenager at the time. Very cut up, from what I hear.'

'What happened to the old man's patch?'

'It got split up. His widow moved away, and we all thought that was the last of the big Malties. Then, about five years ago, Eddy turned up. He'd bought himself a slice of the north end. He was quiet at first, and, you know, just seemed to concentrate on buying out some of the old men. A bit of presh, but not much. Some of it was completely legit, I expect. It was funny having a Malty back – though I suppose he's only half Malty. His mum was pure East End, as far as I remember.'

'Ever seen him?'

'No. You hear much more than you see around here.'

'And what do you hear?'

'Well, first we heard he was a quiet kid. Big and strong but quiet. Then we heard that he was a bit of a joker. Keen on taking pictures. I heard once, a few years ago, he had a false mirror put in one of his tart's flats – she didn't know anything about it. Eddy would let himself in, and while she was earning, he'd take a reel of Polaroids of the punter on the job. Then he'd slip out into the street and when the punter came down the steps he'd stop him and offer him some snaps. The punter usually bought them, as you can imagine. Only trouble was, it didn't do the tart's trade any good.'

'What else do they say?'

'Well, they say he's very grabby. They also say he plans a long way ahead.'

'Has he done any time?'

'Wouldn't know.'

'Got any particular coppers house-trained?'

'Wouldn't know.'

'And what makes you think he's on the move?'

'It's just what you hear. Sometimes you hear wrong. But I don't think so this time.'

'Maybe that's why the coppers are jumpy – they think something's going to break.'

'Maybe. That usually makes coppers excited, though, doesn't it? Nothing coppers like better than villains carving each other up, is there? But the coppers don't seem that sort of excited at the moment. They're just smelling bad.'

'Anything happened so far?'

'Well, bits you can't connect. The thing with Ronnie.'

'How did Ronnie know who it was?'

'Process of elimination. Couldn't have been anyone else. Then there've been one or two bits of nasty lately. A tart got cut up a bit.'

'Sorry,' said Duffy automatically.

'No, no one I knew, but it makes you edgy. And a club

got burnt out – you know, accident, the usual thing. Just happened Big Eddy was interested in the property. Just happened he bought what was left of the building for a little nothing. You see, it's all a bit like that; but you know that if you've heard one or two little things, then you can be bloody sure that other people have heard others, and that they're likely to add up to a move.'

'Who works for Eddy?'

'Lots of people.'

'Anyone in particular?'

'There's Georgiou – remember him? Nick Georgiou?'

'No.'

'Fat guy – ginger hair, glasses, a bit crazy; everyone says don't cross Georgiou. He's a bit sick, they say; likes to make you think he's friendly, then you've got a billiard cue across the kneecaps before you know where you are.'

'Who else? Who does Eddy's dirty?'

'Well, Georgiou likes doing some. Puts in for it. Then there's Kyle. Thin guy, full of mouth. About six feet or so. Very bad teeth. Talks out of the side of his mouth. Very gabby.'

'Anyone else?'

'One or two. Paddick – he's a sort of tough, blond guy. They say he's bent, but everyone's bent nowadays I reckon. Pardon, love. Oh, and Hogan – little Irish guy. Nasty fellow. Grew up throwing paraffin heaters at old ladies.'

'Charming. Where does Eddy hang out?'

'People like that don't hang out, Duffy, you know that. You don't stand around in billiard halls waiting for the Eddies of this world to turn up. He doesn't sit in bars and wait for his runners to deliver. The bars go to him. People like him don't hang out, Duffy, they don't hang out.'

Duffy smiled.

'Well, it's been a good twenty-five quid's worth, Renée.'

'Sixty, love, or I'll be after you with a parry heater.'

'Thanks, Renée, you've been very useful. And to think, I haven't even been here.'

'O.K., Duffy. Just make sure you leave like a punter.'

He left the flat as if in a flurry of guilt, and walked down the alley trying to look like a man who had been tied to a bed for an hour while three tarts in school uniform poured golden syrup all over him and then licked it off. He kept his chin tucked into his neck and didn't look round. If anybody had seen him leaving Renée's flat, he wouldn't have known.

At home that evening, he brought all his artistry and ingenuity to bear on Carol's Cheddar on toast.

'Not bad, Duffy, you're really coming along with your cooking. I don't think I could have bettered this Cheddar.'

Duffy looked pleased. He'd decided to learn to cook after he'd stopped being able to eat cheap copper grub; after he'd got impotent with Carol; after she'd suggested they might still get married and he'd turned away and said 'No'. But cooking didn't come easily to Duffy. Carol kept telling him he ought to develop the right instincts – 'How do you develop instincts?' he asked, puzzled – and his approach was methodical and painstaking. He reweighed flour time and time again to get exactly the specified amount; he scrubbed vegetables as if they had to be clean enough to take part in a moon shot; he regarded every egg and every tin of luncheon meat as if they were explosive devices which had to be defused with the tenderest care.

'It's the mess I don't like,' he had said.

'There isn't any mess,' Carol had answered, looking around.

'That's because I made sure there wasn't.'

Duffy devoted as much time to getting rid of wrappers and packaging the leftover food as he did to cooking. If you opened his refrigerator door, you wouldn't see anything to eat: you'd see shelvesful of opaque Tupperware boxes; polythene bags with neurotically doubled knots in their necks; even, occasionally, Tupperware boxes *inside* polythene bags. The first time Carol took a look, she called out,

'Hey, Duffy, is the food trying to escape or something?' and ever afterwards referred to his fridge as Colditz.

When they had finished supper Duffy washed up at once, in case any germs escaped from the decomposing food and started tunnelling their way into Colditz. Over coffee he asked casually,

'What's going on down at the patch, Carol?'

'What do you mean?'

'Well, you know, what's it like down the station? They jumpy or anything? Anyone getting ready for a move in the patch or anything?'

'Duffy,' she said sternly, 'you don't want to know about that. You're not a copper any more.' Her dark eyes looked at him severely from out of her pretty Irish face.

'I'm interested.'

'Duffy, it's four years. You haven't asked me in four years. We agreed you shouldn't ask. We agreed it wouldn't be good for you.'

'What's going on, Carol?'

'No.'

'I need to know now.'

'No unless you tell me why. And even then probably no.'

'If I tell you some things it might make it harder for you at work.'

'If it looks like getting that way I'll stop you.'

Duffy told her everything he'd learned since that first phone call of McKechnie's which had got him leaping out of bed away from her. He told her the lines along which he was guessing, told her his flickering doubts about McKechnie, told her everything he'd been told by Renée. He didn't disguise the fact that he was as much fired by his

103

interest in Sullivan as he was by earning his money helping McKechnie. At the end, Carol said,

'I don't think I should, Duffy, I don't think I should.'

'Why not?'

'I've lost a lot because of you, Duffy. I've lost four years of maybe being happy.'

'That wasn't because of me, that was because of whoever fitted me up.'

'Same four years, Duffy, same four years. And the black kid may have been a plant, but' – she looked at him reproachfully, for the first time in years – 'you chose him, didn't you?'

'But that was all part of our deal.'

'Well, there's deals you hope will go one way, and deals you hope will go another, aren't there?' Carol sounded almost bitter; she had every right to. She didn't look at him as she continued. 'So now what you're asking me to do is spy on the people I work with, all so that you can earn twenty quid a day from someone who for all you know is a crook. *And* so that you can get your revenge on Sullivan or whoever it was at the station who helped fit you up. Revenge isn't a good idea, Duffy.'

'They say revenge gets better the longer you leave it.'

'Bollocks,' said Carol fiercely. 'Revenge screws you up. You've got to go on living if you don't want to be screwed up. And *I've* got to go on living,' she said with sudden emphasis. 'I haven't had all that much fun for the last four years. There've been some good bits, but I've mainly just been ticking over. And why I keep ticking over is because of my work. I like my work, Duffy, you must remember that, even if we don't talk about it. I may not be keen on everyone at West Central, and I may even have my private sus about some of them, but I'm going to go on working there, Duffy. You screwed up some of my life four years ago, but you're not having another bite at what's left of the cherry.'

'Will you tell me what it's like at the station nowadays?'

'No.'

'Is anyone preparing a move?'

'No. Duffy.'

'Will you tell me how Sullivan's behaving?'

'No.'

'Will you look out the file on Big Eddy for me?'

'No.'

'Then will you do this? Will you – wait for it – will you look out the file on McKechnie for me, because if it turns out you've got reason to know him at West Central then I might just have to pull out of this job, mightn't I?'

'Don't take it as a promise, Duffy, in case it gets broken. All I'll say is if I'm near his file anyway, and there's no one about, and there's no chance of it ever, *ever* getting out that I looked at it, then I might.'

'One last question.'

Carol looked weary.

'Will you stay the night, please?'

Carol nodded, smiled, went off into the bathroom and unsnapped the plastic box labelled 'Watches'.

6

The next morning Duffy made a phone call to an old friend, a specialist at the sharper, technological end of surveillance. Geoff Bell could bug a phone just by scowling at it; could lift a voice-print out of thin air; could lay down a surveillance system which would tell him three miles away if a police dog was taking a leak. He wasn't entirely honest – his moral sophistication lagged a little behind his technological sophistication; though the only time the coppers had tried it on and raided him they got a nasty shock: Bell had so completely bugged and monitored his own flat that three days later he sent them a one-hundred-page dossier detailing what each of the three coppers had done for every second they were in his flat. He even knew that the big, burly copper with the black moustache had approved of the girl's photo that was pinned above the desk. And the day after the dossier arrived, Bell filed suits for trespass, criminal damage and wrongful seizure of property. Somehow the police seemed to lose interest in his case after that.

'Geoff, it's Duffy. I've been in touch with Control and he says could you drop the package behind the cistern in the middle bog as you're leaving Lenin's tomb. The plane tickets will be arriving in the morning.'

'All right, Duffy, I won't record you for once.'

'But you were recording that bit?'

'Of course.' With Bell, documentation was as much a mania as a job.

'And you'll wipe that first sentence of mine?'

'Yes.'

'And then it won't be there?'

'No. Because I'll have wiped it. You slowing down, Duffy?'

'It really won't be there?'

'What's on your mind, Duffy?'

'I've got a tape with a gap on it. Two and a half, maybe three seconds.'

'Nixon's secretary put her foot on the autowipe again?'

'That sort of thing. What I wondered was, do you think you could get anything out of it?'

'Depends. Depends on quite a lot of things. How loud the original recording was. How determined the guy was to wipe it: if he went over it lots of times there probably wouldn't be anything left. Depends if he wiped it on the same machine he recorded it on. Depends how good the tape and the machine were in the first place. Depends how much of a hurry you're in for it as well.'

'Couple of days, would that be enough?'

'I'll do what I can. Most of the time, wipe means wipe, though.'

'Sure.'

Duffy rang off and went and rooted in his tool chest. He found a pair of powerful, short-handled, snub-nosed metal-clippers, and slipped them into his pocket. Then he collected McKechnie's tape, scribbled a note, and put the tape in an envelope to drop through Bell's door. As he ruffled Carol's hair by way of goodbye, she said,

'I haven't seen a thing, Duffy, and I'm sure I wouldn't have liked it if I had.'

'Just a new tin opener, darlin'. Made in Switzerland.'

'Where the nuts come from,' was all she said.

Duffy dropped the tape off at Bell's and took the tube in to Piccadilly Circus. It was beginning to feel like going to work.

He walked up the Avenue, turned left, and approached the Peep Show with his punter's gait. He changed a couple of quid with the cashier, and settled in to a cubicle.

It was early in the day: the Kleenex on the floor was quite dry. He reckoned that the Peep Show probably ran on eight or ten girls. Each girl had about a ten-minute turn, so that they'd have to wait maybe an hour and a half before their next routine. They wouldn't be sitting around in a dressing room with their feet up talking about skin conditioner, that was for sure. Soho was one of those places where time translated directly into money. The old-style whores used to operate like taxi-cabs. You'd have to finish in ten minutes, otherwise they'd start an 'I can't hang about all day' routine; if you wanted another go after you'd finished the first time, the same rate applied, only they gave a discount if you could finish in five minutes.

At a guess, the girls in the Peep Show did a circuit to other such places, or maybe to strip clubs – Duffy wondered if the skin clubs would cease to exist in a year or two – or maybe they popped home and did an hour's trade. Duffy inserted his first 50p piece and the metal shutter slid up. A skinny, underfed girl with tiny tits was dancing as hard as she could, except that it didn't seem like dancing, not compared to some of the others, it seemed more like running on the spot. Round her neck she wore a velvet choker in what seemed a pathetic attempt to distract attention from her waif-like body. Even her pubic hair, Duffy noted dispassionately, seemed lacking in vigour, and grew patchily, with no enthusiasm. When it came to straddling the glass letter boxes, she did it in a wooden, automatic routine, glancing round anxiously to see if she was missing anyone out. Duffy wondered if any of the anonymous circle of eyes found it exciting. He just wanted to throw a Red Cross blanket round the girl's shoulders and feed her some hot soup.

He left his letter box closed for the rest of her act, then dropped in another 50p. Two minutes with his slot open, watching and partly watching; then five minutes or so with it shut. He wondered if punters had to keep up a certain percentage of time with their windows open before they got their doors kicked by the management. Maybe no one minded any more, they made so much money. It was like in the dirty bookshops. In the old days there would be cardboard signs up above the racks of mags saying NO BROWSING. Large men came up to you and said things like 'Two minutes more' and then, with a heavy parody of civility, 'Can I help you?'. Now nobody seemed to care that punters stood in shops for hours on end and then left without buying; the turnover was obviously quite lucrative enough and harassing the customer didn't particularly improve your trade.

Duffy changed some more money, and after he'd got through three quid his slot clanged up to reveal the black girl, Polly. He watched her more closely than the previous girls, checked out the white scar on her shoulder, and then, when she bent right forwards to give the punters a double-barrelled shot, he looked at the top of her thigh: there, right where the thigh joined the buttock, was the pimp's cut: a white scar running down into her groin.

Duffy left at the end of that 50p's worth and waited across the street for the black girl to emerge. When she did, he crossed quickly and caught up with her before she had the chance to disappear like the last time.

'Excuse me,' he said as he came level with her.

'Yeah?'

Duffy didn't know quite how to begin.

'Er, excuse me,' he said again. He felt almost embarrassed; he certainly must have looked embarrassed, because she suddenly gave a hard, professional smile.

'Okay, love, I was going to do some shopping, but I'll fit you in.' She turned round and started walking back in the direction she'd come. Duffy followed, having to catch her up again. She was already rattling off her price list.

'Ten for straight. You wan' it straight? Do you Greek if

you like. Greek's twenty. Blow's fifteen. Hands? Well, hands is ten too, I know it sounds a lot love, but honestly, it's as much trouble as the other. Made up your mind?'

It was only half past twelve. He didn't feel particularly randy. But having got this far he didn't think stopping, explaining who he was, and asking a few questions would produce a helpful response. At her gaff he dropped ten pounds into a little woven basket on a dresser and got on with it. She made a great show of being excited to hurry him along. He made a similar show to fool himself and hurry himself along. Their thoughts were miles away from their bodies.

'There, that's better now, love, isn't it?' For a tart, she was chatty.

'You're Polly, aren't you?'

'If you like.'

'I brought you flowers once.'

She looked at him strangely.

'Listen, love, none of my punters bring *me* flowers. Not even my regulars.'

'No, I brought you flowers in hospital. Four years ago.'

She stopped pulling up her skirt and looked at him again. Then she said,

'Fucking copper, aren't you?'

'Not any more.' He finished dressing and zipped up his blouson.

'I don't take coppers. I never take coppers.'

'I'm not a copper. I'm private now. Can I talk to you?'

'No you fucking can't.' She seemed frightened, even though she was acting angry.

'It wouldn't take very long. I just want to ask you about four years ago.'

'No way. Fucking get out. Get out, copper. FUCKING GET OUT.' She ran to the side of her bed and pressed a bell.

Duffy got out. He got out very fast indeed.

He bought himself lunch at the Casa Alpina, a little

110

Italian café where he sat next to the hatch and listened to the waiters bawling down the intercom. As he sat over the menu a youngish waiter with a bald head and a black moustache rushed at the hatch and deposited a pile of sticky pudding plates in the pulley lift, at the same time bending his head to the intercom and shouting, 'Piccolo hors-d'oeuvre twice!' Duffy liked places like this: the noise, the friendliness, the cheapness. He ordered himself bacon, sausage, eggs, tomato, baked beans, double chips and a half carafe of wine.

He hadn't been counting on Polly, so it wasn't too much of a blow that she wouldn't talk. You just have to try every avenue and hope that some of them lead somewhere. Most of them don't, of course. In any case, he reflected, Polly didn't exactly owe him anything. The flowers had come off police expenses; and he had leaned on her more than a little at the time.

After lunch it was back to the Double Blue. He hoped this bit of the day would go better. He dug out his membership card in the name of Daniel Drough and presented it to the soiled hippy in the box office, who shook his head.

'Sorry, mate, your membership's expired.'

'Don't be stupid, I only joined a few days ago.'

'Sorry, mate, that's not what your card says.' He handed him back the card: Membership for one year from . . . ' it said at the bottom, and on his previous visit the hippy had filled in '10 June 1978'. He'd written '1978' instead of '1979' so that the card appeared to expire the day he had sold it. One of the oldest tricks in the book. Duffy kicked himself.

'Look, you sold me that card a couple of days ago.'

'Me? Not me, mate. I only came back from holiday today.'

'Where did you go?' Duffy was pissed off, especially with himself. The hippy looked mystified. What was this

111

punter doing getting all uppity?

'And besides,' the hippy went on triumphantly, 'this isn't my writing.'

Duffy handed over another fiver.

'Same name again this time is it, guv? Or do you fancy a change?'

'Heath,' said Duffy, 'E. Heath.'

Inside, there were about the same number of punters as before. Twenty or so diligent E. Heaths who might never have moved since Duffy had left the last time. On the screen the beach movie was showing again. Now a fat man had joined the two oily girls, who were toying with a beachball. For some obscure reason – perhaps as a punishment for their lesbian activities on a public strand – he kicked away their beachball, turned them over on their fronts, and began slapping their bottoms. With the amplifying system at the Double Blue, it sounded as if someone were beating carpets: a loud, extended, reverberating crump.

After ten minutes or so of this, Duffy decided to move. He got up from his seat and made his way to the toilet. He walked slowly past it and stopped by the emergency exit opposite the foot of the stairs. He looked up the stairs, listened for a bit, then took out his metal-clippers. He could go for the padlock or he could go for the chain. Both of them were a bit rusty, and almost certainly never used, but Duffy thought it possible that the padlock got a few glances occasionally. He started work on one of the links in the chain. Then he stopped, looked for a rustier one, and started again. After several silent heaving bursts on the clippers, he severed the link at a point where one of its straight sides began to go into a curve. Then he moved the clippers along about an inch and started work again close to the other curve. Soon a short, straight piece of link just under an inch long tinkled on to the stone floor. He picked it up and put it in his pocket.

Next he slowly slid the bolts at the top and bottom of the left-hand door. The door could now be pushed open from the outside until it came up against the chain, which would still hold tight despite the missing piece of link. The exit was in a dark part of the corridor, getting a little faint light from the top of the stairs, and Duffy hoped that no one would take a look at it. It would be just his luck if the G.L.C. decided to send round someone from their licensing department for a spot check.

Duffy walked softly back to the toilet, went inside and shut the door. The cistern had lost its lid at some stage, and Duffy climbed on the seat and peered in. He took the metal-clippers out of his pocket and gently lowered them into the water. The inch-long piece of chain followed. Then he climbed down, satisfied. That was the mechanical side done. The human side was always much more likely to go wrong.

He went back to the stairs and started to climb them. When he got to the top he saw three closed doors. He walked quickly across to the one on his right, the one from which the voices had come before, and knocked. Nothing happened. Instead, there was a voice from behind him.

'Not still looking for the pisser, are we, mate?' It was the big gingery man he'd seen before. 'Because if you are, then all I can say is you can hold it for quite a lot longer than I can.'

He had come out of the left-hand door, and beckoned Duffy across towards him.

'Now, what can we do for you, mate? Not happy with the fillum or something?'

'The film's fine,' Duffy said, 'absolutely terrific. The punters are loving it. They're climbing up their seats with happiness. You're Georgiou.' He hoped to God his guess was right.

'I might be.'

'Going to invite me in?'

'Pardon my manners, squire,' said Georgiou, 'but I'm a bit picky about who I have in my parlour.'

'You don't seem too picky about who you get to collect your drops.'

'Meaning?'

'Meaning the bloke in the denims who did the run from Brewer Street the other day. You must have to tie a ball of string to his ankle or something to make sure he doesn't get lost.'

Georgiou looked at him and grinned.

'I think I might invite you in after all, Mr . . .'

'Wright.'

'Mr Wright? Sounds like it's my lucky day.'

He pushed open the left-hand door and politely let Duffy precede him. Or he could have been making sure Duffy didn't scarper. Duffy went in. It was a small office with a few box files and a girlie calendar on the wall and a little kitchen off to one side. It was reminiscent of McKechnie's office. The main difference was that the pick-up man was lounging on a tangerine settee. Same denims as before; just as scruffy; a half-hearted moustache.

'Take a seat, Mr Wright. I think you'd better have my chair, and I'll sit on the sofa just in case one of the two of you wants to kill the other. By the way, this is Mr Jeggo.' He continued the introduction in formal style. 'Mr Jeggo, I don't think you've met Mr Wright. Mr Wright, I think you *have* had the pleasure of seeing Mr Jeggo.'

Jeggo had clearly heard the conversation on the landing and stared impassively at Duffy. It was the sort of gaze you might run into in an abattoir.

'Mr Wright was just saying, Jeggo, that he thought you could brush up your technique a bit. Weren't you, Mr Wright?'

Duffy judged that there was little to be got from in-

114

gratiating himself with Jeggo; it was probably too late anyway.

'Yeah. First thing I'd say' (Duffy took on the tone of a subaltern running through the mistakes of a squad of new recruits: firm but understanding) 'is that you ought to try and remember which dustbin the drop is being made in. There's no point in Georgiou or Eddy or anyone *asking* for the drop to be made in a precise place and then have the pick-up man acting hunt-the-thimble in broad daylight.'

'You a copper, asshole?'

'No. Second, don't walk along the street to the drop, pick it up, turn round, and walk back from the direction you've come: no one walks down Brewer Street, looks in a dustbin, picks something out and then retraces their steps unless they're a pick-up man. Approach the drop, make the pick-up, and then carry on in the same direction.'

'Asshole,' said Jeggo quietly.

'Third, you did quite right to go up Berwick Street.' (Duffy made it sound as patronising as possible) 'A nun with a wooden leg playing the mouth-organ could lose a tail in that market. But you've got to try: you can't just hope that the market will do the job for you. You've got to *use* it – use the stalls and the people and the way it all works. And the fourth point' (Duffy noticed that Georgiou was smiling to himself) 'is that you'll never spot a tail if you don't look for one. Simple as that. You didn't know if you were being tailed or not; you didn't bother to find out. You just picked up the drop and buggered off home with it.' He turned to Georgiou. 'Oh, I hope you didn't train him, Georgiou. I don't like to seem rude.'

'Not at all rude, Mr Wright. I'm sure Mr Jeggo will do a great deal better next time, eh, Mr Jeggo?'

'I think I'll kill this asshole,' said Jeggo in a toneless voice. Duffy decided to bait him some more.

'Then let's hope you're better at being a killer than you

115

are at being a messenger boy. I wouldn't let you lick the stamps for my letters at the moment.'

'He's a copper,' said Jeggo, 'he reeks of copper.'

'No,' said Georgiou, 'he's too smart to be copper. He reeks of smart, that's all.'

'I wanna kill him,' Jeggo repeated petulantly.

'I don't think that's a good idea, Jeggo. I do think we ought to ask him what he wants first. But we'll bear the idea in mind. Now, Mr Wright, we've had a few laughs, and you haven't come for the pisser, so what's it all about?'

'What's it about is, I don't tell you in front of messenger boys.'

'Very well. Jeggo, go and kill someone in the other room, will you?'

Jeggo got up and left.

'I want to see Eddy.'

'Of course you do.'

'Well?'

'Oh, Mr Wright, I'm merely waiting for you to state your business.'

'I'm from McKechnie. I want to deal.'

'Ah. Well, that's interesting. Would you like to tell me what you have in mind?'

'No. I want to talk to Eddy.' Duffy didn't sound to himself as if he had much of a leg to stand on.

'Well, Mr Wright, Mr Eddy prides himself on the vertical structure of his business. He likes to think that everyone should have access right to the top. I'll go and see what he says.' He disappeared, then put his head back round the door. 'Oh, I shouldn't worry, I don't really think Mr Jeggo means to kill you. It's just one of his exaggerations.'

Three minutes later Georgiou returned.

'Mr Eddy will see you now.'

They went out on to the landing and Georgiou opened the middle door. They were in a short passage, and Duffy

116

immediately felt a change of atmosphere: there was carpet on the floor, and fresh green paint, and a couple of prints on the wall. At the end of the passage was a cream-painted door. It was opened and Duffy stepped through into another world. He found himself in a high, elegant, Georgian double-cube sitting room, painted pale green. There were pier-glasses between the windows and old prints round the walls. The room must be almost twice as wide as the Double Blue below, Duffy reflected; it must run through into the next building, and perhaps the one on the other side too. There were chintz-covered sofas and in one corner a large executive's desk with several telephones on it and a bronze statuette of a swan. The windows were double-glazed, and the pale green carpet was thick beneath Duffy's feet.

Big Eddy Martoff came through a door in the left-hand corner of the room holding a manila file in his hand. He laid it on his desk and walked over to the two of them. He was taller than Duffy; but then, most men were. Still, he was no taller than six foot, and not especially broad. 'Big' was doubtless a street name which had most effect on those who had never met him. He was a good-looking man in his middle-thirties, dark crinkly hair, sallow complexion, brown eyes, high cheek bones above a long expanse of cheek. He was dressed like a man who ran the sort of modern art gallery whose paintings you couldn't afford. A lightweight medium blue suit, soft cream button-down shirt, French tie, expensive mocassin shoes.

'Mr Wright. You like the room?'

'All right.'

'I'm very fond of it. And I'm especially pleased with the Morland prints. I think they suit so well.' He talked like he looked: soft, smooth and expensive. Old Martoff must have left a nice little educational trust for him, Duffy reflected. 'The window seats are very pleasant too,

Mr Wright. Not common in this part of London, as you can imagine. You can sit on one of those window seats and feel the sun on your face and simply forget all about the pressures of business.'

'Hope the floor's soundproofed.' Duffy thought of all the amplified sheepdogs and carpet-beating raging on below. He also thought that, even allowing for a bad tape, there was no question but that Martoff was 'Salvatore'.

Martoff smiled.

'Ah, of course, you came up the back way like a tradesman. I hear you gave a sparkling piece of instruction to one of our trainees on the way in.'

'I think I'll leave by the front entrance when I go, if that's all right by you.'

'Well, let's talk our business first, Mr Wright.' He went and sat behind his desk, beckoning Duffy to a sofa. The sofa felt quite a bit lower than the desk. That corny old executive's trick, thought Duffy; ah well, if he needed it. Georgiou went and parked a fat ham on a window seat.

'Now, Mr Wright.'

'McKechnie says you're squeezing too hard. McKechnie says he's too pressed for funds, business is bad at the moment. McKechnie says will you lay off for a while. McKechnie says what sort of deal do you want from him?'

Martoff laughed lightly. 'Mr Wright, do you realise you started every sentence with the words "McKechnie says . . ." It's like that old game we used to play as children, O'Grady Says. I do hope the same rules apply and that I don't have to do everything that McKechnie says. That would be a severe disappointment to me. What do *you* say, anyway, Mr Wright?'

'I say the same – you're squeezing too hard. After a while you can't get blood out of a stone.'

'Correct me if I'm wrong, Mr Wright, but you haven't come here on a charitable impulse? That is to say, I take it you are not just an old friend of McKechnie's who happened to be passing and was moved by the sight of his distress to come and plead on his behalf? That, I take it, is not exactly the case. You are, are you not, receiving an emolument from McKechnie? Indeed, you are being paid for coming here and pleading McKechnie's poverty, are you not?'

'Not so's you'd notice.'

Martoff smiled.

'Well, let's not quibble. My point is that *you* seem to be getting a bit of blood out of the old stone at the moment. So, for instance, McKechnie could easily give me your blood, couldn't he?' Martoff sighed a little, and stroked the bronze swan. 'It always saddens me, Mr Wright, how much people lie about money. With peasants, well, one expects it; but in business . . . I suppose I'm just a bit too idealistic for my work. You'd be surprised how people squeal that their pips are squeaking when all I have done is gently pinch the peel of the orange between thumb and forefinger, like a housewife at market.'

Duffy waited. With men like this, men used to power, you always let them talk on. Martoff seemed to be coming out of a reverie.

'But then I suppose I am a bit too idealistic anyway. Take the question of you, for instance.' Duffy held his breath. 'I agreed to see you because of what Georgiou said to me. He told me that you had said to him that you wanted to deal. I believed it. So I invite you in, and wait for you to say your piece, and what do I discover? No deal. Nothing like a deal. I mean, what I understand by a *deal* is that one party says, "If I give you x, will you give me y?" and that the second party thinks it over and says either "Yes", or "No", or tries to haggle about the terms. Correct me if I'm wrong, Mr Wright, but as far as I can see from examining your "deal", your "deal" consists of saying to me, in simple terms, "Lay off". Now, isŋ't that

119

what it amounts to?'

'McKechnie says what do you want from him?' Duffy doggedly repeated his only line.

'Oh dear, Mr Wright, I don't seem to be getting through to you, do I? My point is that it's all very well for McKechnie to say his stone is exhausted and has no more blood in it, but what has he got to offer me as a disincentive from having occasional modest stabs at this famous stone of his? That's what I understand by a "deal", anyway. I'm sorry if I'm a little old-fashioned, but I simply see no "deal" at all.'

'Well, I'd better be off then,' said Duffy. He began to rise from the sofa.

'Let me detain you a little longer, if I may, Mr Wright, because there are a few things which it might be in both our interests, not to mention that of your paymaster, to get clear. There are three areas in which I think I could probably help clarify your thinking. I hope you'll bear with me.' He was clearly a man used to being borne with.

'The first is that you didn't come here to "deal". Let's get that straight. You don't have a "deal". I doubt if you even talked about it with McKechnie first, because if you had, then you might have come up with something a little less feeble. So, perhaps you should admit to yourself the real reason for coming. You came in order to see me. I quite understand. I am a local businessman of some standing. A lot of people want to see me. Maybe you thought that unless you invented some "deal", I would not judge you important enough to receive. Well, you may have a point there. But I think we should all remain as clear about our own motives as possible, don't you?

'This leads on to my second point. You were asking, in a rather confused way, about my own motives and intentions in regard to the man whose stone writes so many of your cheques. I think I can be quite open with you, Mr Wright, because if you haven't worked out my intentions by now then you must be as fuddled as poor Mr Jeggo out there. In simple terms – and there are no complicated terms – I am taking over Mr McKechnie's business. That is my intention. If you ask my motive, that is not very shadowy: my motive is that I want to own his business. So, I am dispossessing him of his two warehouses and his office. It is as simple as that. I am sorry if there has been any ambiguity, but I'm afraid my style of business has always been to take things slowly. I like people to get used to the idea of losing their possessions. It sometimes takes them a while to adjust, to make new arrangements. But I'm sure Mr McKechnie will adjust.'

'What if he doesn't want to hand over?'

'Oh, come, come, Mr Wright. Or is that question designed to make me utter some quotable quote? You wouldn't have a tape recorder strapped to your body, or anything foolish like that, would you? We shall be forced to have a look before you go, you understand?'

Duffy grunted. Quite right to dump the metal-clippers.

'Well, the short answer is, that if he doesn't hand over his property to me I shall do various unpleasant and quite possibly violent things which will persuade him to do so; but it would be pushing my current candour too far to tell you precisely what.

'And the third thing is this, Mr *Duffy*.' Duffy looked up, startled at the sound of his real name. He felt his shoulders move and his sphincter contract in a sudden wave of fear. Georgiou chuckled. 'Ah, I'm glad that worked. I do so enjoy surprises. The third thing is this.' Martoff flipped open the file and read from it. '"Duffy. Nicholas, usually Nick. West Central, 1972–5. Average to good arrest record – took in Leverty for a bit, also Spiro, though didn't get a conviction, and Docherty as well. Known to refuse Christmas presents, various kinds tried. Last case – stabbing incident in Bateman Street. Pushy on that one. Dealt with, May 1975. Homosexual, though

121

known to go with women as well. Engaged to W.P.C. Carol Lucas, broken off." My condolences.' Martoff fished in the file and threw a photograph at Duffy. 'Not a very good likeness, is it?' The photo fell to the floor. Duffy bent down and glanced at it as he picked it up. When he looked back at Martoff he found himself staring into a Polaroid camera with a flash attachment. A bulb went off in his face.

'This one, I think, will make our file much more up to date.'

Martoff put the camera down on his desk and came round to the front of it. He sat with one buttock on the edge and looked long at Duffy.

'Two final points. The first is that, though I am not a philosopher, I am sometimes tempted by philosophical formulations. And the one which seems to me most suitable for the current situation I would formulate like this: Knowledge is Power. Remember that, Mr Duffy.' He leaned back over his desk and tapped Duffy's file.

'And the second point, which really follows on from the first point, is this. I am not given to making threats, so you must not interpret my next remark as a threat: it is simply an instruction, a clear, unequivocal instruction, and to make it clearer still I will put it in coppers' slang for you. Get off my patch. Do you understand? You will not return to my area of business operations ever again. You will not upset my employees or trespass on my property or walk the pavements which *I* own ever again.'

'What if I do?' asked Duffy.

Martoff leaned closer to him; the brown eyes stared expressionlessly out of the sallow face.

'Suck it and see, Mr Duffy, suck it and see.'

7

Duffy was thoroughly frisked by Georgiou and sent off back through the Double Blue. They wouldn't let him go down the front steps, wherever they were. As he said goodbye to Martoff, Duffy took a quick, final look round the large green room. In particular, he noticed the wiring high up on the wall above the door from which Martoff had emerged: wiring which led to a little square box painted cream to melt into the background. In the carpeted passage, Duffy stopped to look at a print, and glanced back at the door leading to the green room: nothing there, as far as he could see.

As he headed off down the stairs, Georgiou said to him, 'Hope Jeggo isn't waiting in the pisser for you,' and chuckled.

Duffy rather hoped so too. He had far too much on his mind to have to bother with clobbering Jeggo as well. Not that it'd be much trouble. If you gave Jeggo a knife and told him to kill an old lady, he'd probably grip the cutter by the blade and beat her to death with the handle.

He made his way home oblivious of the light crush of mid-afternoon tube passengers. He was thinking about Big Eddy Martoff. What an inappropriate name it now seemed to him. It was the name of some lunkhead whose hairline came down to his eyebrows and whose hands brushed his shoelaces. Whereas the reality was a person who talked like a member of an Any Questions panel. 'Our team tonight,' Duffy murmured to himself, 'consists of Norman St John Stevas, Richard Marsh, Isobel Barnett, and a newcomer, the London businessman, Big Eddy Martoff.' The name was all wrong: but then maybe it was one of his jokes. He clearly prided himself on his sense of humour.

What Martoff had revealed of himself to Duffy was more than a bit scary. A second-generation Malty, streetwise from his cradle, then sent to some minor English public school to be taught the robber-baron ethics of the British businessman: it wasn't a pretty combination. He was naturally smart, enjoyed his power, and looked forward to enjoying it for a long time more. And he wanted his power to continue so that he could enjoy other things as well: the clothes, the room, both spoke of a man who enjoyed his wealth. That again was the sign of a second-generation villain. The first generation, they're often stuck with the memory of having nothing, so they stay very tight-arsed, very mean: they're the sort of villains who never give donations on flag days and probably keep their money under the bed because they don't trust banks. The second generation always know more about the potentialities of money, are much keener on using the institutions of the legit world to their own advantage. First-generation villains think of themselves as outlaws, outsiders, sometimes even suffer guilt about their social status. Second-generation villains think of themselves as businessmen, protecting and building up inherited capital. Some of them have accountants.

Building up: that was what Duffy was worrying about now. How far did Eddy's ambitions go? He'd appeared to be completely candid with Duffy, and yet he hadn't really told him anything. He was obviously intending to take out McKechnie completely: not just squeeze, but take out completely. Duffy could have guessed that, probably: you didn't open up with a high level of violence unless you were interested in going all the way.

But what about a bigger move? Eddy certainly had the ambition for it, and he certainly had the nerve. He probably had the resources too, in case he had to hire a few out-of-town mercenaries. He'd said that his style of business was to take things slowly; but maybe that was just sales-talk. The most important thing about making a move is being sure of the exact strength of the opposition, and calculating how likely it is that getting active will make that opposition gang up against you.

But hadn't Eddy answered this point? 'Knowledge is power,' he'd said. It was the sort of phoney generalisation Duffy had heard often enough before from villains who fancied themselves, but maybe this time it had a more specific application. Maybe Martoff really did know things. When he'd opened the manila folder and started to read, Duffy had thought it was just a flash trick. One call to a friendly copper or a medium-sized Christmas box to a station filing-clerk and he could have had all that. The folder was just to make it look professional, to make Duffy report back to McKechnie that Eddy knew everything about everybody and that he should just give in, pay up, and move out.

But what if that wasn't the object? What if it had all been an ordinary part of what Eddy constantly referred to as 'business'. After all, he'd known that Duffy was Duffy, so he must have had him spotted at some time. And whose file did it read like – a copper's or a villain's? When it came to the bit about the stabbing incident, Martoff had read out something like 'Pushy on this', and then shortly afterwards 'Dealt with'. That didn't sound like a copper's file. And if it were Martoff's own file, when had it been compiled? At the time of the stabbing? Presumably so, because the photograph was an old one. So how up to date did the file come? Did Martoff know, for instance, that Duffy was Duffy of Duffy Security? Not that he'd need a complex intelligence system to work it out: a glance at the Yellow Pages would do.

And another thing which the file – and the comment 'Dealt with' – meant was that Martoff was admitting that it was he who had fitted Duffy up. 'Pushy on this', 'Dealt with' and 'Homosexual' all added up in Duffy's mind to the Caramel Club and the door being booted in and 'Excuse me, sir, but how old is your friend?' and the fist in the kidneys and the whispered hatred of 'Fucking bent *queer* copper'. So Eddy didn't care if Duffy knew he'd framed him. And having told him in so many words that he'd fitted him up, he then told him to keep off his streets. That showed a lot of confidence. And it left only one question in Duffy's mind about how the Caramel Club incident came to happen: who'd talked on him at West Central? Who'd been the link telling Martoff how to work the frame?

When Duffy got home he telephoned McKechnie.

'Not good news, I'm afraid'.

'What?'

'I've been talking to our friend Salvatore.'

'*Talking* to him? Who is he?'

'He's called Martoff. Big Eddy Martoff. An important member of the local business community, at least if we take his word for it. Has a finger in just about everything by the looks of it.'

'And?'

'And, Mr McKechnie, I'm afraid that what he wants is quite simply everything you've got. It's not just protec. It's the whole way, I'm afraid. He wants your office, your two warehouses, in fact everything you've got.'

'And I suppose he thinks I'm just going to hand it all over, does he?'

'I'm afraid that's exactly what he thinks, Mr McKechnie.'

'And if I don't?'

'Well, from what he says, he will impose a rather severe penalty on you.' It was odd how Duffy found himself almost talking like Martoff.

'So what do we do?'

126

'What do *we* do, Mr McKechnie? I think it's more a question of what do you do? I'm only an employee of yours.' Duffy had decided to stonewall the conversation as much as possible; he'd let McKechnie stew for a bit.

'Well then, what would you advise?'

'There seem to be only three possibilities. You can hand over, you can try the police again, or you can look around for some powerful friends. Those are the normal courses of action. Of course . . .'

'Yes?' said McKechnie hopefully.

'You could always hire somebody to kill Martoff. People in your situation have done that before. But I should advise you it's strictly against the law.'

'I'll get back to you, Duffy.'

'Any time, Mr McKechnie.'

That evening, as Duffy was finishing up a tin of cannelloni, he had an unexpected visitor. A face from the past gave him an uneasy wink from the doorstep.

'Long time no see, Duffy.'

'Well, well, well, this is a surprise. Not the television licence again, is it? It just keeps slipping my mind, officer, I'm afraid. I'll do it tomorrow, I promise.'

'Inviting me in?'

Duffy paused, considered, looked Shaw up and down, wondered what he'd do if he simply shut the door in his face.

'Of course.' Duffy watched him as he came in. Same small, worried, foxy face; the hair a bit greyer now, the suit a little shinier at the elbows, but essentially the same Shaw. He'd never worked directly with him, but knew his reputation: diligent, tended to fret away at a case, largely honest. They always said he was a bit of a puritan. He'd been at West Central almost as long as Sullivan, and yet he was supposed to be still quite shocked by some of the more routine trades of the Golden Mile. Duffy fixed them both some Nescafé and asked,

'How's business?'

'Oh, mustn't grumble, you know. Always a lively turnover. Try to keep on top of it.'

'I'm sure you do. How's the old patch?'

'Oh, much the same, much the same.'

'Good.' Or bad, for that matter. Shaw was acting as if he'd come for a mortgage or something. Duffy eased him along.

'West Central needing an alarm system?'

'What? Oh, no, haha.'

'So what can I do for you?'

'Well, it's a bit awkward, Duffy, but I'll come to the point. Er, I'm here in a strictly unofficial capacity, you understand.'

'No, I don't as a matter of fact. I never understood it when I used to say it. Now I'm an ordinary member of the public, maybe I can ask you to explain.'

'Look, Duffy, there's no point in getting clever. I know you're clever, you know you're clever, so let's leave it at that.' He paused. He looked worried. Eventually he spoke. 'I can say it in two words, Duffy, Lay off.'

'Will you repeat them?'

'Lay off.'

'Who's paying you, Shaw? I ask it in a purely unofficial capacity, of course. Who's got your pisser in his pocket?'

'I'll ignore that remark. Lay off, Duffy, and go back to your burglar alarms. You're in over your head and you don't even know it. Just collect your week's wages and stay away. Trip over something and hurt your foot. Plead industrial injury. You don't want to work for McKechnie. You don't want to go nosing about after Martoff.'

'Leave it to the professionals, eh?'

'And you don't want to start treading on corns at West Central, either.'

'You know, Shaw, I didn't like that red tie much. I really didn't think it suited you. A bit too flash. Not your

128

style at all.'

'What do you mean?'

'The red tie for the café window. I mean, it's gangster stuff, isn't it? All that turning up only two minutes before the drop and having a table reserved for you – it's really not your style, Shaw, not your style at all.'

'We're not talking about style.'

'O.K., let's talk about something else. It wasn't a very conscientious job on your part, I didn't think. I mean, correct me if I'm wrong, but I don't think you managed to hang around long enough for the pick-up, did you, Shaw? Another engagement, no doubt. Pressing business, I'll bet. Skipping off down the street almost before my client's back was turned. Where were you off to – collect your ten per cent?'

'Watch it, Duffy.' Shaw's trouble was, he wasn't good at sounding menacing. He just sounded worried.

'I'm making a strictly unofficial suggestion, of couse. But I'm afraid my client wasn't very happy about your performance, Mr Shaw. And he wasn't very happy either about the lies he got told when he phoned Sullivan for a report. "Ran off into Regent Street and caught a cab", or something like that. If you'd stayed around for a couple of minutes longer, you'd have set eyes on the pick-up merchant and realised that the only way *he* could get a cab to stop for him would be by lying down in the road in front of it. So how much of the three-fifty has come your way and Sullivan's?'

'Duffy,' said Shaw quietly, almost sadly, 'you don't know the half of it.'

'I've used that line before as well and I never understood what it meant. I just used it when I didn't know what to say next.'

'Well, I'll give you just a tiny idea, just a glimmer. Why did McKechnie hire you?'

"Cos he thought I was good, I suppose.'

'But how did he find you?'

'Oh, he said he asked about.'

'And what did you make of that?'

'That my reputation is spreading faster than you think.' It was true, though, Duffy had wondered how McKechnie had got hold of him.

'*I* told him about you, Duffy, *I* recommended you. He came to see me and *I* said *you*. You ask him.'

'I will. Why?'

'It seemed like a good idea then. From what I knew. But I didn't know then what I know now.'

'Well, that's very clearly put. Care to explain?'

'No.'

'What's going on, Shaw?' Shaw didn't reply. 'Is Martoff making a move?'

'I can't tell you, Duffy. I don't know everything, and what I do know keeps changing. What I will say is this. You know as well as I do that in a place like our patch there's always a delicate balance between us and the villains. It's not a great war like the public seems to imagine and it's not a lazy heap of coppers on the take like you seem to imagine. The villains and us carry on side by side and there's a sort of what you call osmosis between us. You understand what I mean by osmosis, Duffy?'

'I understand what other people mean by it as well.'

'Well, you're upsetting this delicate balance, you see, Duffy. That's about as clearly as I can put it to you.'

'You can't put it any more clearly?'

'No I can't. So lay off.'

'What about a deal, Shaw? Everyone's quite keen on deals around the patch, it seems to me.'

'What sort of deal, Duffy?'

'Well, what about this? I'll lay off, as you put it, if you tell me who it was at West Central who fitted me up.'

'Not still worrying about that, are you? It's all dead and past, Duffy.'

130

'Well, if it's dead and past, it won't matter you telling me, will it? Who helped Martoff set me up?'

'I never really knew, Duffy. I had my sus, same as anyone else, but you can't just operate on sus, as you know. Though I can't think who else it could have been.'

'Is it a deal? I'll lay off if you tell me who helped fit me up?'

Shaw paused for a bit.

'O.K., Duffy, it's a deal. But I'd rather you guessed and I nodded my head.'

What difference did that make? So that Shaw could deny having told Duffy? So that he could say Duffy must just have guessed? Still, if it made it easier for his sodding conscience.

'Sullivan.'

Shaw nodded immediately. Duffy picked up their cups and took them to the sink. Then he walked wordlessly to the door and held it open for Shaw to leave.

It was funny. He hadn't minded in the very least lying to Shaw.

He sat and reflected on the odd coincidence of being warned off twice within hours, once by Martoff and once by Shaw. Was there some connection? Had Martoff told Sullivan to send a messenger boy round? What were they afraid he might find out? What was all that stuff about 'delicate balance'? Usually, all it meant was 'Stop interfering with my slice of the take.'

At nine o'clock the telephone went. When the pips finished he recognised Carol's voice, but she didn't say hello.

'I'm not ringing you, you haven't heard from me, you haven't seen me for a week.' She sounded quite calm, as if setting out her terms.

'All right.'

'Your client's warehouse in Lexington Street is burning.'

The telephone went dead. No goodbye, nothing.

Duffy took a taxi, left it in Shaftesbury Avenue, and dodged up Windmill Street through the crowds of punters gawping at the cinema stills. The south end of Lexington Street was cordoned off by police. Half way up he saw a couple of fire engines parked. One had run up a ladder and a fireman at the top was playing a hose on the small one-and-a-half storey warehouse from above. Two more hoses were being aimed on the building from ground level. Duffy wondered if the firemen knew what was inside. There must be quite a danger of an explosion if you had a hangar full of the sort of things kids liked for Christmas: cheap masks painted with cheap, flammable paint; indoor fireworks; paper hats.

Duffy wondered if the coppers had bothered to inform McKechnie. Then he had a thought. He walked along Brewer Street for a few yards and turned up Great Pulteney Street, which ran parallel to Lexington. Half way down it he came to a short alley which went along the side of a pub and was only used by draymen delivering their loads. At the end of the alley there was a fence. Duffy shinned up it and took a look round. He found himself about three houses up from McKechnie's warehouse. The two streets were close together, with only tiny back courtyards between them. Almost all the houses had long since been turned into shops and offices. There were no lights in the windows; everyone had gone home.

The warehouse was still burning brightly as Duffy worked his way gradually across the courtyards. When he got almost opposite he stopped and looked. The flames were stabbing through the roof, despite all the water being poured in by the fire brigade. It was clear that McKechnie's stock would be entirely destroyed. Duffy wondered why Martoff had ordered it: the stock wouldn't be any use to him now; neither would the building. At best, he'd be able to buy up the site cheaply. Maybe that

132

was all he wanted. Or maybe it was simply a move which, like the cutting of Rosie McKechnie, had no obvious motive at the time. Maybe there were payoffs in several directions; maybe people in similar positions to McKechnie were being shown what could easily happen to them.

Suddenly the warehouse caved in. With a long, rumbling roar, the roof gave way. Everything seemed to move in opposite directions at the same time. The roof fell in, the flames shot up, sparks flew in every direction, the rear wall half collapsed backwards and out, and burning bales of McKechnie's goods came hurtling out of the warehouse into the courtyard.

Duffy ran back as the collapse occurred, and waited while the fire took new life with the influx of air. Then, gradually, the hoses began to get it under control again. Duffy walked across to the fence belonging to the office which backed immediately on to the warehouse, and, out of curiosity as much as anything, hauled himself up it. He peered over the top at the burning bundles of McKechnie's goods which had been hurled out by the explosion of heat; the flames were beginning to die down. He looked again. Then he quickly threw a leg over the fence and dropped quietly down into the yard. The only person who might spot him was the fireman on the ladder high above the wrecked warehouse; but even so, Duffy kept in the shadows. A roped cube of McKechnie's goods lay in front of him, about three feet away: it was a charred bundle of magazines. They were not the sort of magazines you gave to a kid in a King Kong mask and a clown's hat.

Duffy reached out a foot and kicked the bundle apart. A few of the blackened magazines on the outside burst briefly into flame again; the rest sprayed out. He read the familiar titles: *Private*, *Colour Climax*, *Selecta*, *Animal No 9*, *Sex Bizarre*, *Ero*. Standard imported hardcore, the secret currency of dirty bookshops. In Duffy's time on the

133

patch, they went for five or six quid a time. He didn't know what to allow for inflation, but he reckoned that he'd just kicked a bundle of five hundred quid or so, in street terms. Big Eddy was right: there was a bit more blood in McKechnie's stone than Duffy had thought.

He climbed back out into Great Pulteney Street and walked down to Brewer. He strolled along to the end of Lexington Street and took another look up it. There were only two hoses on the fire now; it seemed to be coming under control. He wandered on along Brewer Street, fairly certain that neither Martoff's nor Sullivan's men would be giving him a thought. When he reached the end of Brewer he spotted a little knot of gawpers gathered on a corner staring into a dirty bookshop. Not the usual sort of behaviour for punters, he thought. Then he noticed that the shop window had a hole in it and the interior had been damaged by fire. Not gutted – just blackened a bit here and there. Through the window a man in a brown coat could be seen sweeping up.

Duffy chased a memory of five years ago. Hadn't this been one of Ronnie's bookshops? Ronnie, who was Renée's pimp? He checked again in his mind, and was pretty sure it had been. Ronnie in those days had had four shops. This one, one near by in Old Compton Street, one in Frith and one in Greek. Sticking to his punter's gait, Duffy ambled his way along Old Compton Street. Outside the bookshop there he found a shabby fat man taping a newspaper over a hole in the window.

'Get a brick, mate?' he enquired chummily of the man.

'Brick? Fucking paraffin 'eater.'

'Why'd anyone want to do a thing like that?' asked Duffy in a naïve voice.

'Well, it wasn't that Mrs Whitehouse, I can bleeding tell you,' came the indirect reply.

Duffy walked round to Greek Street; as he approached the third of Ronnie's shops the cluster of gawpers round it told him all he needed to know. He went into a pub and dialled Renée.

'It's Duffy,' he said. 'What's happened?'

'What's happened? You've fucking ruined Ronnie, that's all that's happened. Why the bleedin' did I ever let you in? What've you ever done for me, copper? And now you go and lose my Ronnie all his shops.'

'When did it happen?'

'About an hour ago. Heaters through every shop. Frightened the wits out of the punters. All your fault, copper.'

'I'm not one any more, Renée. And how do you know it's got anything to do with me? You said yourself that our friend had already threatened Ronnie.'

'Yeah, well he was going to do only one shop, see? Only you came sniffing to see me. So he rang up Ronnie special, just half an hour ago, to tell him how he had been going to do only one shop, but seeing as I'd been so helpful to you, he'd decided to do all four. So what do you say to that, copper?'

Duffy couldn't think of anything to say, but it didn't matter; Renée put the phone down on him.

He sat in the pub for a bit, wondering about what had happened. It was like a blitz. Was Eddy declaring war in every direction at the same time? And why the old parry heater method? It didn't really work in terms of setting the shop on fire, though it was very sudden and very frightening. It was an old-fashioned technique, used by the generation of, well, Salvatore. Maybe Eddy was being nostalgic, like when he imitated Salvatore's voice; more likely, he found the lapse into barbarism a nice contrast with his green office, his chintz, his window seats, his soft suits.

After a couple of drinks Duffy wasn't closer to any answers, but he had begun to relax. The pub was full; he felt safe. He also felt a bit randy. Maybe he should have

135

pocketed a few of the uncharred mags from McKechnie's Christmas stock. As he sat and thought about it, he definitely did feel randy. It was now almost a week since the future author of the *Good Gay Guide* had dropped his watch into the Tupperware box. Jack had protested that the watch was completely noiseless, the very latest in digital-display quartz technology. Duffy had looked at him sceptically and pointed firmly to the box.

It struck Duffy that one aspect of local life that he hadn't yet checked out was the massage parlours. If McKechnie were as flourishing a businessman as his fire suggested, he could surely afford to treat Duffy to a little body-rub. Every business allows for a percentage of its turnover going in expenses fiddles. Duffy could always claim that he'd spotted Jeggo diving in for a much-needed sauna and had followed him.

He left the pub and looked up and down Greek Street. No time for a consumer survey; besides, he was only a couple of hundred yards away from Martoff's head-quarters. He put on his punter's walk, crossed the street, and pushed open the door of Aladdin's Lamp ('Executive Massage'). In the little front office sat a middle-aged woman in a white nylon housecoat; she smiled at him in a friendly fashion. It seemed to Duffy like going into a ladies' hairdresser's.

'Um, I'd like a massage please,' he mumbled. He hadn't ever used the line before.

'Of course, dear. Do you want sauna too?'

'Er, I don't think so.'

'Well, you can have single girl for eight pounds; single girl topless for ten; two-girl for twelve, two-girl topless for fourteen.' Duffy wondered what the rates included; probably not much.

'How long's that for?'

'Twenty minutes.'

Oh well, in for a penny.

136

'I'll have the two-girl topless please.'

'Very good sir, Number Three, you'll find a towel in there.'

Duffy handed over fourteen quid (almost a quid a minute, he suddenly thought), and went past the woman's desk into a narrow corridor. There were a row of cubicles constructed of stripped pine. They didn't seem very soundproof to him. The lighting was subdued.

He opened Number Three. In the middle was a sort of high narrow bed: mattress, blankets and a top covering of plastic sheeting. A chair for his clothes, with a towel hung over it; a cupboard or two; and a dresser with some oils and powders laid out. He undressed and put the towel round his waist, noticing that it was too small either to go round his waist properly or to cover his pubic region properly. Then he lay down on the bed.

The two girls bubbled cheerfully into the room. They wore cut-off denim shorts and Dr Scholl sandals. One of the girls had small, tight, high breasts; the other larger, more dangly ones; perhaps that was how the pairs went, hedging the clients' bets.

'Oil or powder, sir?' One of the girls was setting a kitchen pinger for twenty minutes.

Duffy couldn't decide. Wouldn't oil take a long time to get off? But powder didn't sound much fun. Oil sounded much sexier.

'Oil, please.'

They turned him over on his front and began to massage him. One concentrated on his shoulders and back, rubbing oil into him and dipping her tits down every so often and rubbing them against his back; this was the girl with the larger tits, and he certainly knew it. The other girl worked on his legs, getting ever and ever closer to his groin. He felt his erection getting squashed between his thigh and the bed.

Then they turned him over on his back. As they did so,

the towel seemed to fall half off him and his erection lurched sideways into view.

'Oh, what a naughty boy,' commented the girl down that end. 'What have we here?'

Duffy didn't feel he needed to answer that one. The girls continued working on him with their oil and their breasts. The way the oil got wiped off his body on to their breasts seemed very nice indeed to Duffy. Everything, in fact, seemed very nice to Duffy, especially the way the girl down the bottom end was getting nearer and nearer his cock. Every so often her forearm seemed to brush it, nudging it into ever harder erection. She didn't actually touch his cock, though. He remembered vaguely that there was some legal nicety to be performed before they would actually wank him off. Yes, that was it: the client had to propose the idea. Duffy wondered at the form of words. Eventually he tried,

'I'd like you to go on doing that.'

Quick as a flash the lower girl replied, without stopping her handiwork,

'You want relief?'

Of course, that was the phrase, Do you want relief? He nodded.

'Relief's ten.'

He pointed at his pile of clothes, and the girl at his head went over, rummaged for his wallet, and showed him the two five-pound notes she was taking. Meanwhile the lower girl took a dollop of oil and started smoothing it into his cock and balls. Ah, that was bringing him some relief already, he felt. The girl at the top end started rubbing her tits enthusiastically over his chest.

'I think it's time for a nice surprise,' said the girl at the bottom end, 'so close your eyes.' The girl with the big tits helped him by holding her breasts over his face, running them up and down a bit and then settling the nipples softly on his eyelids. Even when the girl at the other end

138

momentarily stopped rubbing him, his cock still pulsed and soared. He heard a cupboard door click open, then shut, and wondered what she was doing. Maybe she was getting out a box of tissues.

The larger girl's nipples were pressed tight against his eyes. The girl at the end pulled a couple of times more on his oiled cock; then he felt something being gently slid round the base of his balls. Maybe some oriental device to make coming more exciting, he thought.

'You can look now,' said the girl at the bottom end. The nipples were removed from his eyes and he looked down the length of his body. What Duffy saw then was the most frightening thing he had seen in his whole life.

Looped around the base of his cock and his balls was a thin copper wire. The wire met and crossed over itself where his cock joined his stomach. At each end of the wire were wooden handles; the slimmer girl was holding one in each hand. It was a garrotte. She said to him very quietly,

'Don't move, copper.'

The other girl went across and pushed open the door. In walked Big Eddy Martoff. He was smiling.

8

Eddy gently took over the wooden handles of the garrotte from the massage girl. He nodded his head towards the door and the two girls went out. Eddy went on smiling.

'What about my ten quid?' asked Duffy. 'My ten quid for relief?'

'Oh, this could give you relief from everything,' said Eddy softly, 'from absolutely everything.' He tugged very gently on the garrotte.

'And another thing,' said Duffy, acting anxious in an attempt to stay cool. 'Why does everybody keep calling me "Copper"? I'm not a copper, you know that. Why did you tell them I was a copper?'

'Such semantic niceties, Mr Wright. At a time like this, too. I don't think the girls would have enjoyed having you on so much if I'd told them that you were only an ex-copper. I don't think they would have put their hearts into their jobs quite as much. I trust, by the way, that there was nothing wrong with the service you received up to the moment I came along?'

'Absolutely no complaints,' said Duffy. 'I'll always come here again.'

'I'm so glad.'

Eddy looked down at Duffy's groin. Depleted by fear, his rig now lay like a large snail, its head flopping sideways across his thigh.

'Well, we do seem to have lost our enthusiasm, don't we?'

'What about my ten quid?' said Duffy. It was the only way he could keep his mind off horrifying possibilities.

'I think that's the least of your worries.' Eddy, equally,

was determined that Duffy should keep his mind on horrifying possibilities; he tugged gently on the handles; the thin copper wire bit slightly into the base of Duffy's cock, and gathered his balls up tighter together.

'Now, Mr Duffy, you have bought cheese in your time, I expect?'

Duffy had.

'Then I expect you will remember how they cut cheeses. Not the soft cheeses, but the hard cheeses. Cheddar, Cheshire, that sort of cheese.'

Duffy did.

'Well the wire they use for that is the same wire which is currently threatening to do you a serious injury.'

Duffy thought about foot-high barrels of Cheddar being sliced vertically in half. Even enfeebled old ladies on the cheese counter didn't break sweat. The wire just slipped through the Cheddar as if there were no obstacle at all. Duffy wasn't sure that he would ever be able to face cheese on toast again.

'Now, Mr Duffy, I admit that meat offers rather more serious resistance than cheese. All those sinews and bits of muscle and veins to sever. But I'm sure we'll discover that roughly the same principle applies. What's the betting I could tug your tassel right off with one pull?'

Duffy had run out of complaints to take his mind off what was happening. He lay there silently, staring at Eddy's powerful wrists, at his fingers on the handles.

'You do realise, Mr Duffy, I hope, that if I pull these handles it will be curtains for you? I don't just mean that you will be kissing your dubious masculinity goodbye. You will be doing that, of course, without question. But you will probably die as well. Did you realise that?'

Duffy croaked a quiet no.

'Oh, yes indeed. You see, the area I am, what shall I say, hovering over, is one of the major nerve centres of your body. Normally the body is quite unable to cope with the

141

severing of the genitalia. Quite unable. The shock is simply too enormous. Very few people have ever survived such an event. Of course, it's possible that by warning you in this way, your body will have the opportunity to build up some resistance to the forthcoming shock. But I'm not an expert on the nervous system, so I'm afraid that I can only hazard this opinion.'

Duffy wanted to vomit; he wanted to shout Sadist, Murderer, Shit, Bastard, Fuckpig, and anything else that came into his head. But he was unable to utter a word; his eyes simply remained fixed on the backs of Eddy's hands.

'I suppose the general public would probably approve of my action if they saw it as removing a homosexual from the community.' Eddie was in a musing vein. 'After all, I don't really believe that a lot of the legislation Parliament gives us is a reflection of popular demand. For instance, the people have never been in favour of the abolition of hanging. Yet Parliament decided that hanging should be done away with. I call that fundamentally undemocratic, don't you, Mr Duffy? Oh dear, we have gone quiet, haven't we? So what about homosexuals, Mr Duffy? I mean, do you really think that most people in this country *approve* of homosexuality? I don't. I think most people in this country think it's disgusting. But does our Parliament understand this? No. And why? Because, of course, our Parliament is stuffed with bents who are frightened for their jobs.'

'In the same way as Parliament is stuffed with murderers who are frightened for their necks?'

'Very good, Mr Duffy. I was beginning to be afraid that this was turning into a monologue. Yes, you're quite right, my comparison does not extend all the way. But I'm sure I'm right about the homosexuals in Parliament. I remember one I was at school with. Frightful fellow. Always off behind the cricket pavilion. He's an M.P.

now – completely safe Tory seat somewhere up in hunting country. Now if his constituents knew, I bet there'd be an awful scandal.' He paused, and seemed to ponder. 'You see, what chaps like you don't understand, Duffy, is that the British people hate bents. They really do. Think of all the nasty names they have for them. There aren't any nice names, are there? Give me a nice name, Mr Duffy.'

'Gay.'

'*Gay*?' Eddie chuckled. 'You don't look very gay to me, Mr Duffy. You've never looked very gay to me. I shouldn't think you looked very gay when the coppers had to come and kick your door in to rescue that poor unfortunate youth from your clutches. I understand he was a black kid as well. That does seem to me to be taking a very unfair advantage, Mr Duffy.'

'Was he working for you, Martoff? Or did you sub-contract?'

'I couldn't possibly tell you a thing like that. Anyway, I don't employ queers.'

Not even twenty-five year old black ones who look younger and can act like the Royal Shakespeare Company, thought Duffy.

'Still, I don't want to get drawn into discussing the wider social questions which might be raised by you being bent. We could go on all night once we embarked on such subjects. One issue simply leads on to another.'

'Has anyone ever told you you ought to go on Any Questions?'

'What a charming thought. I wonder how you get on to the panel?'

'I think the normal way is to blackmail a few radio producers and stab their wives.'

'Duffy, you are a witty fellow. You know, I'm rather enjoying our conversation.' Eddy smiled again. He was a keen smiler. 'But anyway, I suppose, since I seem to have you currently rather at a disadvantage, that I'd better ask why you are still soiling my pavement with your presence? I thought I told you, quite plainly and clearly, to avoid walking on *my* streets.' Eddy wasn't smiling any more. 'I seem to remember instructing you in copper language, so that even you would be able to understand, to get off my patch.'

'You burnt down my client's warehouse,' said Duffy.

'Ah,' said Eddy. 'I think that's rather jumping to conclusions, don't you? I should imagine that if there were a third person here, I could probably sue you for slander. Yes, I'm sure I could. Not that I'd get much money out of you, I suppose. You haven't got private means by any chance, Duffy?'

'You must be joking.'

'Well, I am really. So there wouldn't be much point in suing you. I'd merely end up with my own legal costs to pay. Suing you really would be like trying to get blood out of a stone.'

'What did you want to burn McKechnie's warehouse down for? You won't get any money out of him that way. All those King Kong masks and novelties and hats going up in smoke. I can't understand you, Eddy. What sort of money do you think McKechnie can get for a load of charred kids' toys?'

It was the only way Duffy could think of to play it. Not exactly play the innocent, that never fooled anybody. But play the smartass who doesn't really know as much as his opponent. People enjoyed outwitting smartasses.

'Duffy, I repeat, I did not "burn McKechnie's warehouse down". Unless you want to get into trouble we had better adopt the formula "McKechnie's warehouse burnt down". The intransitive mood, please, it's much less contentious.'

'Well, now that his warehouse has burnt down, he's going to have even less money to pay you off with. I can't understand why you did it – sorry, I'll rephrase that – I can't see that the sad loss of one of my client's warehouses will produce any immediate benefit for you.'

'Very well done, Mr Duffy. I'm talking of your language, of course, not your thinking.'

'What's he got now? Just another warehouse packed with toys and novelties. That's all his capital assets. Plus a rented office. You might make him, I mean, he might decide to scram and, er, sell out to you. But what good is a burnt-out warehouse to anyone?'

Suddenly Duffy saw what he should have seen earlier. Insurance. Of course, that was it. When he first set up business he used to tell clients that the best security they could buy themselves was insurance. Naturally, McKechnie's stock would be insured. So, instead of pushing for a hundred quid a fortnight or whatever, Eddy helps McKechnie liquidise half his assets in one go by burning down his warehouse. McKechnie gets the insurance money, and Eddy demands it all, presumably under threat of something very nasty happening. Eddy also agrees to take over the lease of the warehouse, or what is left of it, on terms not too disfavourable to himself.

The only trouble with this idea was that the warehouse was full of porn. Insurance companies would hardly pay for the replacement of *that* stock-in-trade. So McKechnie wouldn't get any money. No: more likely, Duffy realised, was that only parts of the warehouse were full of porn. McKechnie probably ran a legit business as well for the sake of cover. Most of them did. So what happened if his warehouse burnt down was that he got compensated by the insurance company for the loss of his legitimate stock, and – with a little encouragement from Eddy – he got prosecuted by the coppers for his cache of *Colour Climax*. McKechnie ended up with cash to hand over to Eddy and got the push from the coppers at the same time. And all for the price of a box of Swan Vestas. If that was how he'd worked it, it was bloody clever. But would Eddy have known what was in the warehouse beforehand? Well, his slogan was 'Knowledge is Power'; Duffy wouldn't have put it past him.

The last thing Duffy wanted to do, though, was let on to Eddy what his guesses were. His best hope was to carry on playing the dimwit smartass to the end.

'Or maybe you want to build on the site of the warehouse?'

It was the sort of idiot's suggestion which appealed to Eddy. He chuckled to himself.

'I'm afraid you simply don't understand business, Mr Duffy.' And then, indulgently, 'I might want to build on it at some future date, yes, that could be a possibility.'

Eddy appeared to be thinking. His grip on the garrotte slackened a little. The wires round Duffy's rig relaxed a bit.

'I think I must consider what to do with you,' he finally said. 'My father always told me as a boy that a rushed decision was usually a wrong decision. I shall have to think about you for a bit, Duffy. You'll bear with me, of course. Georgiou,' he shouted.

The door opened and the plump ginger head of Eddy's Number Two appeared. He smiled at Duffy.

'Still looking for the pisser, mate?'

Duffy shook his head.

'Go through his clothes.'

Georgiou searched Duffy's clothes and pronounced them clean. The garrotte was carefully unwound and he was ordered to dress. Duffy vaguely thought of rushing them, but the possibilities of success seemed slim. They seemed even slimmer when the door opened again and Jeggo came in.

'Ah, Mr Jeggo,' said Eddy, 'been out practising our pick-ups, have we?'

Jeggo scowled. He produced a pair of handcuffs.

'Yes, Mr Duffy,' said Eddy, 'I'm afraid we're going to have to handcuff you to take you to, well, to somewhere else. Would you put your hands behind your back, please?'

Duffy did as he was told. Jeggo clipped the handcuffs on and racked them up tightly. As he did so he whispered into Duffy's ear,

'Kill you, asshole.'

'Jeggo,' said Georgiou, 'you're not threatening Mr Duffy, are you?'

Jeggo turned round.

'Copper in cuffs,' he said, and laughed.

They led Duffy along the passage past the other massage cubicles, and out through a back door. Duffy looked around him – it was a change to discard his punter's droop – and worked out where they were going. Across a courtyard, through a garden, past the back yard of a pub – that must be the Duke of Hamilton – left through a gate, and out into another garden, flagged this time. They walked him across to a back door, through a kitchen, up some stairs, and pushed him ahead of them into a side room. There were three beaten-up armchairs in it, plus a table; a calendar with a view of the Lake District hung at an angle on one wall.

'I really must do something about the furniture in here,' Eddy commented. 'It's just too depressing. And the lighting. We must stop all this central lighting we've got everywhere, Georgiou.'

Georgiou nodded in agreement. He waved Duffy across to an armchair. He and Jeggo took the other two, while Martoff closed the door and went away. Jeggo was in the armchair immediately opposite him, staring at him with a sort of contented hostility. Duffy felt he just wanted a rest after his ordeal in the parlour. He didn't feel like baiting Jeggo. In any case, it hardly seemed fair to bait Jeggo. In two meetings he'd revealed a vocabulary of barely a dozen

147

words, at least five of which were the same word: 'asshole'. While he was thinking about this, Jeggo suddenly revealed a new corner of his vocabulary.

'You a Norman?'

Duffy hadn't been looking at him and didn't pay any attention to the remark. Jeggo got up slowly and kicked him on the ankle. Then he sat down again and repeated,

'You a Norman?'

Duffy looked across at Georgiou for elucidation. Georgiou smiled. It must have been a trick he had caught from his boss.

'I think you'll have to explain,' Georgiou said.

'You a Norman?' Jeggo repeated again. 'A Norman Scott? You queer, copper? You are queer, aren't you? Whatcher wearing that earring for if you aren't queer?'

Duffy didn't reply. None of the standard replies seemed appropriate, and with his hands manacled behind his back he didn't feel much like provoking Jeggo into taking free kicks at his ankles.

'Hey, Georgiou, the copper's a Norman. We've caught ourselves a Norman. Haw, haw.' For the first time in their brief acquaintance, Duffy noticed Jeggo showing signs of pleasure. He was becoming positively lively. Almost companionable. 'I wouldn't be in your boots, copper. Mr Eddy doesn't like Normans. He doesn't like coppers much either, but he *hates* Normans. I bet he's thinking up something really special for you. Haw, haw.'

Duffy didn't reply. He also tried to keep his mind off the garrotte.

'Shall I tell him, Georgiou? Shall I tell him some of the things Mr Eddy's thought up?'

'If you like, Jeggo, we've got time to kill.'

'We've got assholes to kill as well.' Jeggo seemed to be reverting to his more usual theme. Duffy waited. There wasn't any alternative to waiting.

'I remember we had a Norman once. We let him run a

little restaurant. Our mistake, really. What did he do? Hired a load of queers as waiters. Proper lowered the tone of the neighbourhood, it did.' Duffy wondered where Jeggo himself had to go in order to raise the tone of any neighbourhood. 'Still, for a bit we said it takes all sorts. Bit soft he was on Normans in those days, Mr Eddy. So what happens? He falls behind with his payments. Well, we did put them up a bit on account of him bringing all these queers into the district. So, anyway, he doesn't pay. Asks for a bit of time. So we go in and we do a little damage. Not much, you know, but I suppose we did put the wind up a few of the customers. They all ran out into the street shouting about how to get soup out of their lace frillies.

'So anyway, this Norman decides he's had enough, and he asks Eddy to buy the lease back off him. Well, Eddy gives him a fair price, though it's not very much, because well, the place was a bit broke up, and anyway, he didn't exactly have much goodwill to sell, did he? So Eddy's a bit disappointed, you know, I mean he's a bit sour at the way this particular piece of business has gone. So he finds this geezer, very pretty guy, Norwegian I think he was, off a ship, and he slips him a few notes and sends him off to the restaurant. Well, the Norman who runs the place, you should see his mouth water, he really thinks it's his lucky day. The pools have come up, he says to himself.

'What he doesn't know is what Eddy knows. So he gives this Norwegian fellow a slap-up meal on the house, and then they flap wrists at each other, and then he takes him home. Three weeks later he starts getting a bit itchy. Then he starts pissing razor blades. Then he goes down to the clinic for Normans and finds out he's got the worst case of syph they've seen in years. In three places, too.'

Jeggo seemed really happy. He chortled, looking pleased that Duffy had dropped in. In case anyone had missed the point, he summed up, 'He doesn't like Normans, Mr Eddy doesn't.'

'Oh, really?' replied Duffy.

They sat in silence for a while, until Eddy put his head round the door and summoned Georgiou.

'Keep Mr Duffy entertained, will you, Jeggo?'

There was another silence. Duffy hoped that Jeggo's idea of entertaining him was to leave him alone with his own thoughts. It wasn't.

'I can't remember any other Norman stories offhand,' he said, 'but I remember a very funny thing Mr Eddy did to a squealer once.'

'I'm not a squealer,' said Duffy, hoping to head off the story with logic.

Jeggo looked cross; he'd been interrupted before he could get into his full narrative flow.

'You're a copper, though.' Why couldn't they learn around this place, Duffy wondered. 'Coppers and squealers are about as bad as each other.'

Duffy let that one go.

'We had this squealer once,' Jeggo began again. 'Now, if there's one thing we hate in our business it's squealers. We hate Normans a lot, but not as much as squealers. Now, if we could find a squealer what was *also* a Norman . . .' Jeggo seemed to come over all dreamy.

'Anyway, we had this squealer once. He was an Irish fellow. Nice boy, but a squealer. He tipped off a rival firm about a nice big lorryload of books someone was bringing us. Don't know why he did it. Must of been the money I suppose. Anyway, a couple of the lads picked him up and they brought him back to see Mr Eddy. Mr Eddy was pretty cheesed, I don't mind telling you. I mean, nobody squeals on Mr Eddy, and that's a rule.

'But Mr Eddy didn't do anything on the spur. He likes to think a lot before he does things. A big thinker, Mr Eddy. So after he's been thinking for a while, he

150

comes in and he sends me out for a tube of that super-glue. You know what I mean? Bonds in seconds. Says on the packet you've got to keep it on a high shelf, 'cos otherwise kids get hold of it and stick all their fingers together. And then you have to take them down the hospital.

'So I gets this glue and bring it back to Mr Eddy and we go in to see this Irish boy. He was shitting himself, you can imagine. Mr Eddy was quite careful really. Course he struggled a bit, once he saw what was coming. Mr Eddy puts the glue all over his lips. So he pulls his lips right back. So Mr Eddy puts some glue on his front teef as well. Then we pushes his mouf together.'

Duffy winced. It was presumably Eddy's way of making the punishment fit the crime.

'And now we come to the good bit. You see, Mr Eddy wanted to make the Irish lad understand what he'd done. I mean, he'd lost us a lot of books. It wasn't just the squeal-ing, it was the loss of business Mr Eddy minded. There was a lot of books in that lorry.

'Now the Irish boy was, how shall I put it, well, he wasn't a Jew, understand what I mean? We took him into a room, and he was holding his face in a funny sort of way, but otherwise he was all right, and one or two of us held him down a bit, and then Mr Eddy, well he believes in the personal touch, pulled down this Mick's trousers. Then he got his little bit of flesh and pulled it down a bit and glued it all together. Like they say, bonds in seconds, takes two elephants to pull it apart. It all looked so neat, we just had to have a giggle. And the Mick, he just looked down at himself. He was really beginning to sweat, I can tell you.

'What he didn't know was that it wasn't going to get any better. We cuffed his hands behind his back – I fink they may be the same bracelets you're wearing – and took his trousers off altogether, and then took him into another

151

room. Big Eddy had really thought about it. The room had nothing in it except for books – you know, magazines. All spread out and opened up, they were. Just the sort of stuff he'd lost us. And we locked him in there. Think of that – wherever he turned there was nothing but tit and beaver and cum-shots. And you can't keep your eyes closed for ever. And even when you do you can't stop where your mind's going.

'I don't fink he liked it much. I fink if he'd stayed there longer than he did he'd of gone crazy. But after a day or so, Eddy decided to let him go. Put him in a car and dropped him outside a hospital. I don't fink the Mick squealed again.'

For the second time that evening Duffy felt like vomiting. It wasn't the violence and the craziness which made him feel bad. It was the awful strand of logic which ran through what these people did. The sort of logic whereby the victim is persuaded that there's some sense in the violence that is being inflicted on him. There was another reason why Duffy felt like vomiting. He didn't think that the evening was over for him yet.

'Mr Duffy, are you feeling all right?' Eddy had come back into the room and was leaning over him. 'You haven't been abusing him, have you, Jeggo?'

'I been telling him what we did to that squealer Mick.'

'Oh dear, yes. Well, let me put your mind at rest, Mr Duffy. I don't think it's going to be an evening for the glue. I hope your strength will keep up, though, because I think we might have a bit of a night still ahead of us.'

They took him out of the room and along a corridor. As they went through each door, Duffy scanned the doorframes. At the end of the corridor they hit carpet. Carpet and sporting prints. Duffy flicked his eyes over one as they passed. A country gentleman was sitting beneath an oak tree after a hard morning's shooting; he cradled a long-barrelled musket in the crook of his left elbow and knee; one dog lay sleeping at his feet, another was bounding on to his right knee, eager for more killing; on the ground beside him was a careless pile of dead rabbits, made bloodless and picturesque by the artist. Duffy read the caption: 'Rabbit Shooting – La Chasse aux Lapins'. Printed with the export market in mind, he reflected – just like today's porn mags, whose brief texts came in four languages.

Through another door and they reached the Georgian double-cube room. Duffy was led, still handcuffed, to the sofa. As he was about to sit down, Eddy suddenly stopped him.

'No, no, that must be very uncomfortable, sitting like that. We'll put them on you again from the front. You won't, of course, struggle, or do anything silly.'

'Can I rub my wrists a bit?'

'Of course. But I think we'll sit you on the sofa first. It's very hard to surprise people when you're sitting on a sofa.'

They sat him down and crowded round him while they undid the cuffs. He rubbed his wrists for a couple of minutes, then held them out forwards.

'Perhaps not quite so tight, this time,' Eddy instructed. Jeggo looked disappointed. 'After all, we're not dealing with Houdini.'

Then he dismissed Jeggo and told Georgiou to stay. Duffy looked round the room again, ostensibly to admire, really to check the doors and windows. The latter were hidden by full-length chintz curtains which matched the sofa and chairs. Brass standard lamps supplied the sort of light Eddy was presumably hoping to install in his other rooms. Duffy wondered, not for the first time, at the way in which this graceful, genteel room, the prints, and Eddy's elegant clothes were subsidised and maintained by punters peering through glass letter boxes, by the amplified wailings of sheepdogs and Hoovers, by thousands of copies of *Hogtie* and *42-Plus*. He kept such thoughts to himself.

'Very pretty,' he simply murmured.

'Yes, indeed. Now, Mr Duffy, it's already midnight, but I'm afraid we're going to have to detain you for quite a bit longer. An hour or two, probably. I hope no one is expecting you back?'

Duffy didn't reply. Eddy watched him from across the top of his desk.

'Of course, your private life is no business of mine. Still, I should think that most of the late-evening customers of the Aladdin's Lamp would, on balance, probably not be going home to bed-partners, if I can use as neutral an expression as possible. Georgiou and I occasionally have to work as late as this, though we always try and let our wives know in advance. We certainly let them know we would be working late tonight, though of course until you turned up we didn't know quite how late we might have to stay. But then, that's business. By the way, Mr Duffy, did you register the appropriateness of the name I chose for the Aladdin's Lamp? I hope you found it as witty as I do.'

Duffy hadn't actually thought about it. He doubted if many of its other patrons had either.

'Now, Mr Duffy, I propose to be fairly frank with you. I trust that you will be equally frank in return. I am, of course, more than a little displeased that you took my instruction to stay away from my pavements so cavalierly. But now that I have you here I would like to take the opportunity for a little exchange of information. We like to keep our files up to date. Now, you left the force some four years ago, as we have already discussed. What have you been doing since?'

Duffy didn't know how much Eddy might have on his file that he hadn't revealed in their previous meeting, so he played it reasonably straight.

'I set up a security firm. Advising businesses about how to vet personnel, that sort of thing.'

'Oh, I see. Quite an appropriate profession. What other sort of things?'

'Well, I tell them how to set up scanning equipment to stop pilfering, that sort of thing.'

'Ah, we may have to come to you for advice one day. At the moment the punters in the shops are much too timid to try running off without paying. That is one advantage we have over other businesses. And how is your firm doing?'

'So-so. It's a bit seasonal. A big rush of crime always helps.'

'How ironic. You depend on crime for your job. I depend on silly laws and public prudery to keep my business ticking over. But Mr McKechnie, when he came to you, didn't come for a scanning system.'

'No. He wanted me to find out who was preshing him.'

'And why did he come to you?'

'He knew I did a bit of freelance work on the side when trade was slack. I was recommended to him.'

'And you found out who was preshing him?'

'Yes. You.'

'And you told him who it was?'

'Of course.'

'And what did you tell him he should do?

'I said he had three choices: give you what you want, have another go to see if there was a straight cop at West Central, or look for some powerful friends.'

'Perfectly sound piece of thinking. And what did he say in reply?'

'He said he'd ring me back.'

'And did he?'

'No.'

'And did you suggest any other alternatives to him?'

Duffy considered. A sudden suspicion came to him.

155

Maybe their conversations hadn't been entirely private. He said lightly,

'I told him he could always try and kill you. But I warned him it was against the law.'

'So it is, Mr Duffy. I'm glad you pointed that out to him. I wouldn't want him running away with any wrong ideas. You didn't suggest yourself for this project?'

'No, I didn't suggest it seriously.'

'And did McKechnie indicate to you whether or not he might go looking for some powerful friends?'

'No.'

'Do you think he has any?'

'I wouldn't know. I shouldn't think powerful people would be interested in the friendship of a bankrupt importer of King Kong masks.'

'Well put, Mr Duffy. So, in short, would you say that the task for which McKechnie hired you is complete?'

'I suppose so.'

'No lingering reservations? No pricking conscience?'

'No.'

'Good, Mr Duffy. I think you've been very frank with me. Franker, if anything, than I expected. Now I'll tell you a thing or two. You have, if I may say so without sounding patronising, done very well in your investigation. You seem to me to have worked diligently and efficiently. Since we first became aware of your presence you haven't done anything to draw attention to yourself unnecessarily. Indeed, the first time you were pointed out to me in the street by Georgiou, I said that you looked just like an ordinary punter. As a businessman, I admire that professionalism.

'You've found out various things, and you've reported back the knowledge you have obtained. You understand in a small way what I practise in a big way. I think I explained the previous time we met my philosophy that knowledge is the basis for power. And the corollary of that is that your small piece of knowledge can be easily neutralised by my much larger amount of knowledge. Your small piece of power obtained through your investigations can be rendered entirely harmless by the considerably greater power I obtain from my considerably more thorough researches. Why do you think great men have always established great libraries? Because they understand the secret of power.

'Don't look at me like that, Mr Duffy. Just because I talk of great men it doesn't mean that I have delusions of grandeur. You'd like that, of course, it would make it all much neater for your copper's mind, wouldn't it? On the contrary, I have no claims or ambitions to be a great man of any sort. I am a successful businessman with very precise business aims. I obtain the knowledge I need for the implementation of those aims.'

It all sounded so reasonable in this easy, sanitised language. Duffy had difficulty reminding himself that the 'business aims' involved things like paraffin heaters through Ronnie's windows and a Stanley knife on Rosie McKechnie. He also couldn't work out whether or not Eddy was telling him any secrets: whether he was giving away a lot, or giving away nothing.

'You see, let's take the present case. Yourself. Now, many businessmen in my position would react extremely unfavourably to your presence, even to your existence. I should think your average local businessman, put in my position, might react rather sharply. Wouldn't you agree?'

'Depends how smart they were,' said Duffy.

'Oh, come come, there's no need to try and flatter me. What I am going to do with you has been entirely decided, anyway, and you couldn't possibly change my mind about it. No, we are talking in general practical terms. Now, the average local businessman, having already warned you off his patch as I did only the other day, would undoubtedly take it as a severe affront to his sense of machismo that you

157

returned. He would also – rightly or wrongly – feel that what you had found out was a threat to him. So he would naturally be extremely unpleasant towards you. This unpleasantness would doubtless express itself in violence. In some cases, the scale of the violence might be such as would result in your death.

'Now, I am not necessarily against such drastic measures in business terms. And if I made such a business decision about you, there wouldn't be much trouble implementing it; I'm sure you'll agree, if you think of Jeggo's quite severe hostility towards you, that there wouldn't be any problem of implementation. Well, this particular course has been urged in your own case, but I have been inclined to take a different line. Why eliminate, I always say, when you can neutralise? Why be so proud of your knowledge and not use it to the full?'

Eddy suddenly got up from behind his desk and disappeared into his side room, the one with the tiny cream-coloured box perched just above the door. He came back with several manila files under his arm and sat down next to Duffy on the sofa. He tapped the first file.

'Now, this one will be familiar to you already.' He opened it and Duffy saw it was his own file. 'Updated, you see,' said Eddy, and pointed to the latest Polaroid of Duffy. It showed him sitting exactly where he sat now, holding in his hand the earlier photograph from the file.

'Quite an ironic picture, don't you think? I suppose we could take another now of you sitting looking at a photo of yourself looking at a photo of yourself. Like those mirrors set in parallel where your image recedes for ever.'

He put Duffy's file down and tapped the others. 'It wouldn't be a good idea to let you see all of these, but I'll show you enough to tantalise you.' He flipped open the first and Duffy saw a bundle of photos of Ronnie; Eddy quickly flipped through the papers beneath: reports, transcripts of telephone conversations, Xerox copies of

Ronnie's letters, a sketch map, photos of Renée and several other tarts. It looked at least as full as the sort of dossier West Central would have on Ronnie.

Eddy opened the second file and chuckled. Duffy looked at the first photo; after a while he said, 'My God,' and Eddy chuckled again. It was McKechnie's secretary. She wasn't wearing her silver cross and she wasn't wearing her long skirt. She wasn't wearing any skirt. Or knickers. Or anything. She had her hair done in a different style and looked as if she was about to bounce on stage at the Peep Show.

'One of yours?' asked Duffy.

'Trade secret,' said Eddy. 'Not that it matters. I think she might well have a bad case of 'flu by the time it comes for work tomorrow.' He opened the third, thickest file, and said, 'I think it might be a mistake to let you see more than the photos in this one.'

Duffy looked.

Sullivan! Sullivan blurred, walking down a street. Sullivan in beach shorts on some possibly foreign beach, surrounded by businessmen, also in beach shorts, none of whom Duffy recognised from his days at West Central; they were all raising their glasses to the camera. Sullivan in a restaurant with Eddy, and looking round very crossly at a candid cameraman's sudden flashgun. Sullivan looking much younger – maybe twenty years younger; that was interesting. Sullivan with someone who just possibly might not be a tart on his arm. Eddy closed the file, and moved on to the next.

'And the next I probably shouldn't show you at all.' He merely turned the file sideways and showed Duffy the name down the spine: McKechnie.

Eddy gathered up the files and took them back into the side room. Then he walked to his desk, picked up one of the phones and pressed a button.

'You ready? . . . Yes . . . Good . . . Two minutes.' He

looked up at Duffy. 'And now, Mr Duffy, while you think over the implications of what you have just seen, you're going to find out the difference between being eliminated and being neutralised.'

This time they blindfolded him, took him along the corridor they had come in by, and down some steps; they turned him round on the spot so many times he was giddy, then walked him a bit, took him up some steps, out into the open, back indoors, along a corridor, past somewhere hot, and eventually got him to lie down on what felt like a high bed. Then they pulled his manacled hands up over his head and tucked them behind his neck. (Was that why they had handcuffed him more comfortably in the green room?) He heard a faint clink and discovered he couldn't move his hands. Then his shoes and socks were removed, his trousers and pants taken down. He lay quietly; there was little point in kicking out if you were blindfolded and had your hands manacled behind your head. Two people took him one by each foot, pulled his legs apart a little, and tied some sort of straps round his ankles. He felt helpless, exposed, felt that he was going to be castrated.

Then they simply cut the clothes off the top half of his body. He felt a large pair of shears snipping up the arms of his blouson, then up to the neck, and the garment fell of him in three pieces. His shirt was sheared away from him. Now he was completely naked and strapped down. Some-one laid a couple of cloths – perhaps towels – over the straps restraining his ankles. His thoughts chased their own tails round his head. And all this time no one had uttered a word. It made the isolation worse.

And it made what happened next feel odder. He smelt something sweet quite close at hand. Then he felt some-thing damp being poured on to his stomach. Then a hand began to massage oil gently into his stomach. Then another hand joined it and began to spread the oil up to his chest. Shortly afterwards another pair of hands began to work on his legs. Every so often he felt tits brush gently against him. Then something different from the previous time in the Aladdin's Lamp happened: a mouth lowered itself softly on to his cock and began to lick.

If the body could obey orders of the mind, his cock would have stayed the shrunken, tiny, timorous object it had been all the way up to this point. But the body is fractious, temperamental, disobedient. Duffy knew this from his night with Carol: how many times had he sworn at his recalcitrant flesh? And this time, though his mind was tense with fear, his body relaxed. As oil was rubbed smoothly into his cock, it grew and prospered. Tits grazed softly over his chest, then went away. His cock was being wanked with the gentle firmness of a professional. He felt flesh ease itself between his knees – perhaps the girl who had been at his chest was now kneeling between his legs. The silence continued, broken only by the soft swish of oiled flesh. He felt a fresh touch on his cock, and then, from darkness and silence, the world suddenly, horribly roared into light and sound.

It took Duffy perhaps five seconds from the blindfold being withdrawn for his eyes to get used to the light, and to see what they had done to him. And in five seconds a Polaroid fitted with a Powerwind can take maybe half a dozen pictures. The ones which Eddy took after the first six were probably not of much value to him, for Duffy let out a roar of pain and anger, his face contorted, and Jeggo had to punch him very hard in the ear to shut him up. But the first half dozen, with the angelic, flaxen-haired, seven-year-old boy grasping Duffy's erection, and Duffy himself, his arms crossed behind his head in the posture of a sybarite, looking up with a puzzled stare of pleasure – those six would do for Eddy's purposes.

They untied Duffy and told him to collect his clothes. He put on his trousers, shoes and ripped shirt, and folded

161

up the three bits of his blouson. They kicked him out of a side door and he stood on the pavement in Frith Street with tears trickling down his face. A cruising taxi passed but refused to stop for this weeping scarecrow who was probably just another Soho drunk. Sick to his stomach, Duffy set off to walk home.

9

Duffy got home as light was breaking and the first milk-men were clinking their way on their rounds. He looked through his kitchen window at the clock wrapped in polythene. It said two minutes past six. He fell on his bed and slept without a murmur, without a dream. It was when he woke that he had the dreams, and found his present flicker-lit with jagged flashes of the night before. Of the whirr and splut of the Powerwind Polaroid disgorging its prints. Of Eddy, Georgiou and Jeggo hanging over them while they developed, giggling like school-boys at their first X-film. Of Eddy turning and saying to him, 'Don't go away, we may need another set.' Of the child between his legs, looking as if he had just been set down in a grand sort of playpen. Of the two girls who had wanked him suddenly coming over all maternal with the child, who had started crying when Duffy began roaring. Of Eddy's smile of triumph, knowing that he didn't even need to explain the angles to Duffy. And of Eddy's final gesture before they booted him into the street – reaching across and tucking into Duffy's shirt pocket the least useful of the prints.

Duffy suddenly had a thought. Maybe the picture showed him being hit by Jeggo. Maybe it showed hand-cuffs. Maybe he could take it to the police, to some police somewhere, and show that it had all been a put-up job? He dug out the photo, looked at it, choked, and despaired. There was no ambiguity about what the picture showed: a masochist paedophile who liked being chained up and beaten while a young boy held his cock. Given the context, Duffy's open-mouthed roar of pain translated as the expression of a deviant reaching climax.

Duffy screwed up the photo and threw it in the waste-paper basket. Then he dug it out, took it over to the stainless steel draining board and put a match to the edge. The white cardboard caught slowly, then burned towards the edge of the print. Duffy half expected it to go out when it reached the chemicals, but it caught more fiercely, with enthusiastic flame and gouts of black smoke. Bubbles ran across the surface of the print ahead of the flames; the photograph curled and bent as they started to die. Duffy sniffed the deep black smoke; the fumes smelt of burning oil refineries in a distant land.

All day Duffy sat with his body roaring hotly for revenge, and a cool, wise voice inside his head telling him that there was nothing he could do. Big Eddy had neu-tralised him, as Big Eddy had neutralised Sullivan and Ronnie and even that secretary of McKechnie's who looked like a religious maniac but had a Peep Show body. Duffy wondered about Sullivan, about how they had ensnared him. A long, slow business, no doubt, a gradual putting-together of evidence, a deliberate recording of what would seem to the outside world like little favours but which to Sullivan may have seemed innocuous, and may even have been innocuous at the time. Take the photo of him eating with Eddy. Perhaps Sullivan had been invited to lunch by a third party: an informer, say, or someone with whom he dealt. They sit down to lunch – maybe they're going Dutch, or maybe Sullivan's paying – have a few drinks, and after a bit Eddy arrives and greets the stooge in a chummy way. What do you do if you are Sullivan? Get up and walk away? So Eddy sits down, you set a glass in front of him, perhaps he has a snack to keep you company, and suddenly the flashgun of a passing restaurant photographer goes off in your face. Do you get up and arrest him? Eddy seems as upset as you are, chases the man out, comes back saying how bad for his business the photo could be. And so you forget about it. Except that the photo ends up in Eddy's file, and what does it show now? A West Central Super having a friendly lunch – all wine and camaraderie – with one of his patch's top villains. Somehow, the stooge is obscured by Eddy's body in the picture, and it looks as if Sullivan and Eddy are lunching tête-à-tête.

And after that it gets easier. Easier for Eddy, and, in a way, easier for Sullivan. Soon you stop being certain where your world ends and the villains' world begins. You even begin to meet Eddy socially: you think you might be able to get something out of him. He might get drunk and let something drop. Of course you have to get drunk in order to encourage him to do the same. And what does a cigarette lighter matter: you needed one anyway; it's hardly a bribe, is it? Of course it's not a bribe – it stands to reason. What copper would risk his job for a cigarette lighter – *therefore*, it cannot be a bribe. Even if it is inscribed. And then, maybe, you take a holiday with one or two fellows you've met drinking. A bit of abroad, shake the dust off your feet, look at the pretty girls on the beach, have a few jars, well, maybe we won't take the wife, say it's an Interpol conference or something. And Eddy turns up; had business in the area, thought he'd drop in. Joins in the fun, good company Eddy is, life and soul, have a few drinks, a few photos, and then maybe, well all the other chaps are doing it, Eddy's doing it, it seems churlish not to, you have yourself a bit of local girl. The girl's very nice to you, doesn't seem to mind that you don't parliamo the old italiano, doesn't seem to mind that you're a bit fat and a bit drunk and that you don't do it all that well. And then Eddy bids you all goodbye, wouldn't like to embarrass the Super by arriving at Heathrow with him, pop off now, byeee. And he goes. But it all ends up on Eddy's file, and however it was, however Sullivan knew it really was, it can only look the way it looks on Eddy's file.

And after the meal, and the holiday, and the girl, and the cigarette lighter, it all gets easier and easier. The favours come: maybe Eddy feeds Sullivan the odd villain or two; after all it's in *his* interest to see that Sullivan remains a successful local copper. Not *too* successful, of course, in case he gets transferred, so Eddy feeds him mainly minnows; but he helps keep him in business. And then, gradually, comes the payoff, or rather the beginning of the payoff, because it goes on and on and on, and will keep going on, until there's no more paying to be done. It's none of my business, Ernest (they'd be on Ernest and Eddy terms by now), but from what I hear I think you've got the wrong chap in that little case where the pimp got cut: I've been asking around and this is what I've come up with – and then evidence so good any copper would buy it, release his suspect, and arrest the man Eddy decided to fit up. And Eddy would keep your telephone calls on record as well.

And so it goes on. Oh Ernest, I'm having a little local trouble with some new fellow called McKechnie. I don't know what you've got on him, but I'll send you round what I know; he's a bit of a trouble-maker from what I hear. I shouldn't think he'd be a good influence on the patch. And then a bit later, Ernest, funny thing happened, you know, I had a little chap come to see me today, quite a bright little fellow. Face from the past, I expect you'll remember him, name of Duffy. Yes, that's right, yes, queer. Bright fellow, but, well, I think he's getting into the wrong company, Ernest. He seems to be doing some sort of job for McKechnie; no, I'm not sure exactly what, and I'm pretty sure he doesn't really know what McKechnie's up to. I mean, I don't like to see a fellow like that get into any trouble, even if he is a queer copper we had to get rid of; I was just thinking maybe you might send someone round to have a word with him? Straight away? Oh, no need to hurry, Ernest, but, well, now you

come to mention it, that would be quite useful. You've
got his address, have you? Good.

Duffy didn't find corruption hard to understand, and it
didn't make him priggish either. Anyone could go the
way of Sullivan, and then live for twenty, thirty years
making little payoffs here and there, bending things just a
bit, justifying it to yourself by keeping up your arrest
record – and all the time there would be a sort of tape-
worm inside you, feeding away in your guts. It wasn't
guilt, and it was too imprecise to be fear; it was a sort of
hideous worry, a nagging certainty that one day you'd be
called on to deliver too much, one day it would all be put
in black-and-white terms instead of these comforting
neutral greys, one day Eddy would be there flourishing all
he knew about you and saying, 'Fucking do this or I'll
break you.' And you knew that if you didn't do it, he'd
break you; and if you did do it, you might get broken by
someone else, but there was just a chance that you might
get away with it and that it wouldn't show, and it was
always the better chance to do what Eddy suggested. So
you did it, and this time it went wrong, and you were
busted, broken, chewed up and spat out, sent down for a
few years while your wife had to handle the shame and the
loneliness and the sudden loss of your pension; what
she'd married wasn't after all a successful Soho gang-
buster but a fat convict who'd never really been very nice
to her, who'd lied and gone off on holidays with criminals
and slept with foreign whores and now, at the end of his
career, wasn't even going to bring her home a pension.
And how are you going to face the neighbours with *that* in
the papers, Mrs Sullivan, without a trip to the doctor's and
talk of stress and the change and a bottleful of little pills
and then, well, Ernest isn't going to start seeing how fast
the sherry's going down now that he's in the Scrubs, is
he?

That was one of the points about corruption: you never

167

thought of the side-effects at the time. As you clinked glasses and climbed into your beach shorts, you didn't really think about a Stanley knife tracing a three-inch cut down the right shoulder blade of Rosie McKechnie, who may have been married to a pretty shady fellow, but being married even to a murderer isn't a crime yet, is it? That's the sort of connection you don't make, you don't think cause-and-effect operates in that way; and yet it does, it's exactly that sort of equation which in the end is presented to you, maybe in court or in your head, though usually by this time you're head's so muddled it can't even follow simple equations like that. No, your head says, it wasn't *me* that cut Rosie McKechnie, you can't blame that on *me*, I was miles away, I was at my desk, no, I was even arresting someone at the time. You may have been, but that was only cover.

Duffy understood Sullivan perfectly; and understanding him didn't make him feel morally superior; but it did make him feel free to hate Sullivan with all the rage at his disposal. Because one of the little cause-and-effect links Sullivan might or might not understand any more was that it was he who had destroyed Duffy's career. Sure, Eddy set it up, set the black kid up for Duffy; sure, it was because Duffy was after Eddy that Eddy did this; but without Sullivan as informant, as tip-off man, as maker perhaps of that final phone call to the Paddington police – without Sullivan, all you had was a villain trying to frame a copper. Not much headway usually made there. Sullivan it was who made it work.

And now Duffy had gone back to his old patch and got caught in Eddy's net all over again. And Eddy, like a great big spider, had neatly trussed him up, injected him with something which made him quite harmless, and let him go. Eddy knew that the scraps of information Duffy had gathered were valueless compared to one corner of a single snap that Eddy had taken last night. As he was

168

booted out into the night from the side door into Frith Street, Duffy, the tears welling in his eyes, had mumbled to Eddy that he'd come back and break his cock off. Eddy had chortled back at him,

'Suck it and see, Mr Duffy, suck it and see.'

And the three men had giggled, as they'd giggled when they'd watched the Polaroids gradually developing.

Duffy wanted to ring Carol, but he wasn't sure he dared. He wasn't even sure she'd believe what he told her. He wasn't sure he ought to sleep the night with her ever again after what had happened. The last time Eddy had fucked him up he'd been left unable to make it with Carol; he'd been left a compulsive one-night-stander, a user of whores and casual trade, bruised and wary when it came to emotional contact. What would be the result of Eddy fucking him up again this time? He didn't like to think.

He tried not to think of lots of other things during the rest of that day. He roamed around his flat, fed casually, walked the streets, dropped over to his office to see if there was anything on the answerphone, went home, watched five solid hours of television and collapsed into another dreamless sleep. Not surprisingly, since all the horrors came to the surface naturally enough during the daytime.

The following morning he tried to kick himself into working. He pulled out some plans of offices and tried to give himself tests, asking how he would fit the cheapest and most efficient scanner network, or alarm system, given the particular area and its problems. The trouble was, he didn't really care. All he cared about was what was going on underground in his mind.

In the course of the day he got three phone calls, all of which helped him come to a decision. The first was the briefest.

'Oh, Duffy, it's Brian McKechnie here.'

'Fuck off, McKechnie.'

'I beg your pardon?'

'I said, Fuck off McKechnie.'

There was a vague, spluttering noise at the other end.

'Oh, McKechnie, don't ring off. There is one thing. Is your secretary in today, by any chance?'

'My secretary? Why? No, she isn't as a matter of fact. She's got 'flu. Some sort of summer 'flu, I suppose.'

'Thank you. Now fuck off, McKechnie.'

Duffy put the phone down. The second call came in about lunchtime. Duffy had almost forgotten about it. As he picked up the phone, he heard a thick Russian accent.

'Meester Daffy, ees yor controll. You weesh to yoin Keem in Moskva thees week orr nechst?'

'Geoff, hi. What is it?'

'What is it? Only the little job you gave me. Nixon's secretary with her foot on the autowipe – remember?'

'Sorry. Of course. No, I had a bad night's sleep last night.'

'Are you sitting comfortably?'

'Yes.'

'Then I'll begin. I take it the tape you sent was recorded on a Sony portable SK 6500?'

'I don't know; well, I know it was a Sony.'

'Well, it must have been an SK 6500 then. Fortunately they don't rub out that well – the manufacturers often assume that on these little portables you'll never just want to rub out so that you get absolute silence, you'll only want to rub out when you re-record over the top. And the guy who wiped it – who I presume is the same guy who is speaking in the bit that's erased . . .'

'Can't tell you, Geoff. You never know who might be listening.' Duffy always liked teasing Bell about his paranoia. Bell never noticed.

'Quite right. Anyway, the guy who wiped it used the same machine that he recorded it on, which wasn't the thing to do if he was really keen to lose it. And it doesn't look as if he knew about these machines because he only went over it once, I'd say.'

Bell stopped. It was the techniques of finding things out that fascinated him much more than what could actually be found out by using such techniques. Duffy prodded.

'That's terrific. And what did you find?'

'Ah, that took a little while. The traces weren't perfect, I had to re-record, blow it up, break it down – shall I tell you exactly what I did?'

'I'd rather hear what was in the gap.'

'Ah.' He sounded disappointed. 'Shall I tell you over the phone?'

'Let's risk it.'

'I don't like that word "risk". Never use it myself. Well, the sentence, let me get my transcript, the sentence read, "I'm not having some GAP GAP GAP coming on to my patch and telling me how to run my shop." That was before I filled it in.'

'Yes, Geoff, and after you filled it in?'

'Ah, let me get my other transcript . . . "I'm not having some grubby ex-fiddler from up north coming on to my patch and telling me how to run my shop." I had a bit of difficulty getting "grubby" out of the tape, but I'm pretty sure that's what it is.'

'No doubt about the rest?'

'None at all.'

'Thanks very much, Geoff.'

'What shall I do with the tape?'

'Could you possibly deliver it with the transcripts to an address I'll give you? Today.'

'Well . . .' Geoff sounded doubtful.

'I can't tell you why, I'm afraid.' That clinched it.

'Of course.'

The third phone call came late in the afternoon, when Duffy was already rooting in his work cupboard for supplies. As he picked the phone up, he carried on checking the set of screwdrivers, the plastic-handled pliers, and the cutting knives he might need. He heard the pips panicking, then Carol's voice came on. Like last time, she didn't identify herself.

'I'm not going to repeat it. Born Brian Kelly, 1929, Newcastle. '49 London, '52 back north, Leeds, Manchester, Newcastle, '73 London. '51 receiving London. '53 receiving Leeds. '54 receiving Leeds. '61 indecent material through the post Manchester. '65 Obscene Publications Act Manchester. '70 receiving Newcastle. Probation, six months, six months, fine, three months, one year. Released '71, clean since, and don't ask me ever to do this again Duffy are you all right?'

'I've got to see you tonight, Carol.'

'Sorry, Duffy, I've got a date.'

'No, I mean got to, Carol. Got to. Please cancel it.'

There was a silence.

'I've never asked you to cancel before. It's always been part of the agreement, that I'd never ask you to cancel. I'm asking now. I'm serious, Carol.'

'O.K.'

'Your place, please. I'll be late. Probably very late.'

'I don't want to hear why, Duffy. Just don't tell me why.'

'I won't. And thanks.'

Carol hung up. Duffy went on with his quiet, methodical preparations. He laid everything he might possibly need out on the table, and then selected in order of probability of need. There was no point setting off festooned with equipment like a fucking Sherpa. He might as well carry a large sack over his shoulder labelled Swag.

He wondered about the best time. Everyone said two in the morning was the best time. Duffy thought it was a rubbish time. Two in the morning is when sounds travel for ever, when a sticky window makes a soft squeak and three Panda cars hear it from miles away. Two o'clock is when insomniacs look out of their windows and long for an excuse to phone the police, just to talk to somebody, anybody. 'Oh, officer, there's a rather suspicious cat on the roof next door. It's got four legs, a ginger coat and is carrying a jemmy.' Two o'clock is when the burglars who get caught go burgling.

Duffy settled for ten thirty. Lots of punters still on the streets, the pubs still going strong, lots of stray noises drifting about. The tarts getting into double figures for the day.

He wore an anorak with pockets all over it, jeans and soft-soled shoes. He went in by tube as usual to Piccadilly Circus, strolled slowly along the Avenue and put on his punter's walk as he turned up a side street. He worked his way across to Greek Street, crossed to the east side of the street to avoid walking past the front window of the Aladdin's Lamp, crossed back, and went into the Duke of Hamilton. He bought a half of lager and went out into the tiny garden at the back. It was a cool night, and the only people there were a couple sitting at a table holding hands. They didn't pay any attention as Duffy walked to the farthest table and sat down. They didn't pay any attention as Duffy sipped his drink slowly and watched them out of the corner of his eye. When the barman called Time and they dragged themselves out of each other's eyes, they didn't even notice that there was no one else in the garden with them.

As he sat in the shadows of the courtyard behind the Double Blue he realised that he had miscalculated. There were no lights at all in the upstairs windows; but downstairs the cinema was still going strong. Easing their way out of a back window and floating towards him came the noises of amplified pleasure: the sounds of wailing sheep, and of bats being bludgeoned to death.

173

At eleven the noises stopped. At eleven ten the lights were turned out. At eleven thirty Duffy thought it was time to move. He pulled on a pair of very thin, transparent rubber gloves, got up out of the shadows and walked quickly to the cinema's emergency exit. He listened for a moment with his ear to the door, found himself uttering not exactly a prayer but a profound wish, and pushed gently on the right-hand door. It opened an inch, two inches, then the retaining chain was pulled taut. Duffy paused, fished in a pocket, took out a pencil-thin piece of metal about three inches long, and tugged on the end. Three sections telescoped outwards, until he had an instrument about a foot long. He poked this through the gap in the doors, pulled the right-hand door almost shut on the metal rod, and moved it slowly upwards until it touched the chain.

By closing the door Duffy had relaxed the chain as much as it was possible. He pressed upwards on the chain, his eye squashed against the eighth-of-an-inch gap between the doors. Nothing happened. He pressed again, then started jiggling the chain up and down with his rod. Suddenly the cut link freed itself, and the two ends of the chain swung down, the one on the left striking the metal door with a clang.

Duffy listened, then pushed very gently on the door. He squinted through again. The padlock was clearly attached to the right-hand bit of chain, the bit he couldn't see; but its weight meant that as he pushed, the section of the chain that was gradually freeing itself, clinking slightly as each link ran over the rail of the push-bar, was the part he could see, the left-hand end. What he wanted to avoid was the whole end of the chain swinging free and falling away to hit the other door. Duffy pushed until the door was about six inches open, then decided on another course of action. He pushed his rod through one of the links of the left-hand chain, and simply began to lift. This

174

freed the chain and at the same time eliminated the danger of part or all of it falling loose.

When the chain came free of the push-bar on the left-hand door, Duffy pressed on the door until it was wide enough open to let him through, then slipped inside. Quietly he replaced the chain as it had been before, fitting the cut link back into place. Then, being doubly – maybe unnecessarily – careful, he slipped the bolts on the open door back into their slots.

After the lager and the nervous wait until the Double Blue closed, what Duffy needed most was a piss. He knew it would only be on his mind if he didn't have one, so he walked down the corridor towards the cinema and found the toilet. He debated whether to leave the door open for more light, or close it for better sound-proofing. Eventually he pushed the door to, lit his tiny pen-torch and pissed carefully against the side of the bowl. Then he climbed up on to the bowl, fished in the cistern, and collected his heavy, snub-nosed metal-clippers. No point in leaving more evidence on the scene that you had to.

He dabbed the cutters dry on the thigh of his jeans and walked quietly up the stairs. He got to the landing and was about to open the middle of the three doors when he suddenly noticed a light coming from beneath the door of the room on the right. Then he heard a slight banging and shuffling noise, followed by a distinct cough. Fuck it. Damn. He wondered if someone was sleeping the night there. Or perhaps they were just locking away the takings from the Double Blue. All the doors opened into the rooms from the landing, which didn't help Duffy. Eventually he decided to wait pressed against the wall by the side of the right-hand door. He waited there for five minutes or so, then heard footsteps approaching.

As Jeggo put his head out to look for the light switch on the landing, Duffy hit him as hard as he could on the side of the head with the metal-clippers. Even the shortest

175

fights are noisy. Jeggo roared with pain, and Duffy hit him again nearer the temple with the cutters, grunting loudly with the effort as he did so. Jeggo fell to the floor about as quietly as an entire sack of coal being emptied down a metal chute into a coal cellar.

Duffy had knocked enough people unconscious to know that they didn't necessarily stay that way for as long as you wanted them to. He took Jeggo by the back of the collar, and carefully avoiding the blood which was staining the right side of his face, dragged him through the middle door and along the carpeted passage. He flicked a light switch, climbed on a chair, and examined all the surrounds of the door-frame at the end of the passage. It was clean. He turned the handle and found it was locked.

First he squinted through the keyhole to find out whether there was a key left in the lock. There was. Then he extracted a little probe with a magnet on the end which snapped on to the snub end of the key and allowed him to manipulate it. The magnet wasn't strong enough to unlock the door with the key; but strong enough to turn the key itself to a vertical position, so that he could push it gently backwards until it fell out on to the carpet on the other side. Duffy then took out his set of skeleton keys and had the door open in a minute.

He dragged Jeggo through into the green room and dumped him on the floor. He bled quietly on to the carpet. The curtains were closed, so Duffy turned on one of the lights, the brass standard lamp nearest to the side room. Then he pulled a chair over to the door and climbed up on it. With his pen-torch pressed close to the cream-painted box, he examined every edge of it, found some screws which had been crudely painted over, and with a short screwdriver chipped away at the hardened paint. Then he slowly undid the screws. As they loosened, he pressed against the cover of the box. The screws fell to the floor, and the lid was held in place simply by his hand. He laid his face close to the left-hand side of it and very slightly pulled the cover away on that side. Then he did the same on the right-hand side. He couldn't get at the top, so he ran a thin blade between the top edge and the wall. Again, nothing. He couldn't get at the bottom edge because it was tight against the top of the door-frame. This was the big one you simply had to risk. Duffy looked round to make sure he'd worked out the quickest way to the door in case there was a trigger on the bottom edge. Then he gently began to lift the cover away.

Nothing happened. Nothing happened except that, when Duffy looked at the alarm he nearly giggled. Then he did giggle. Jackson and Horwill had started making these in 1952, and for some reason had kept them in production until the mid-1960s. They weren't bad – that's to say, they went off reliably, they made a loud noise, they didn't need servicing – it was just that, well, burglars practised on these when they were still at primary school. They were the sort of alarms which villains taught their wives how to defuse, just so they could get a feeling of what hubby's job was like. There were hoary burglar's stories which turned on getting to a job with the very latest equipment and finding yourself faced with a Jackson and Horwill '52.

Two minutes and a few keys later, Duffy had opened the door to the side room. As he did so, he heard a sound from the floor. Jeggo was moving a bit, making a little noise. Duffy walked quickly across and kicked him on the side of the head that was nearest him – the side that didn't have blood on it. If that fucked up the inside of Jeggo's head, he thought, it could only be an improvement.

The room was very neatly arranged. On the far wall were the manila files, covering about three shelves. A to Z. He reached up to the top shelf and pulled out 'Duffy'. In a pocket on the inside of the left-hand cover were the

Polaroids from the night before last. He put the file on one side. Then he looked for one or two names in particular. Then, on an impulse, a sudden, slightly sick impulse, he looked for Carol. Thank God, she wasn't there. He looked for Shaw. There was a very thin file, a photo or two, nothing much, a few notes, as if either they hadn't tried to get anything on him, or else he was one dourly honest copper.

Duffy pulled out the rest of the files and tipped them on to the floor. Tightly packed papers burn poorly, so he scattered them loosely. Then he looked around the room and noticed two metal filing cabinets. Locked, but Duffy could open them blindfold. One was full of cassette tapes, again filed in alphabetical order. He went through them slowly. The other had a number of 8 mm. cine-films in it. He broke one open, went back into the green room, and held a strip up to the light. Then he piled the films and the tapes on top of the manila files.

He took his own file, opened it up and placed it flat on the carpet. He took out the Polaroids and built them into a house of cards. Then he took a box of matches and lit the edge of one of them. It caught, the edge burned, and then with a sudden flare the chemicals on the print surface lit. Soon all the prints were alight, and papers round the edge were beginning to catch as well. He watched unblinkingly while the Polaroids bubbled and flamed, and started giving off smoke and the smell of burning oil. He watched them curl and bend, and then the house of cards he had made collapsed. More papers caught, the fire was well alight; Duffy fed on some tapes and films, then some folders, and decided it was time to leave.

He propped open the door into the side room to help ventilate the fire. Then, as he left, dragging Jeggo with him, he propped open each door in turn. Already as he left the green room he could feel the heat of the fire. He dragged Jeggo bumping down the stairs, pulled the chain out of the emergency exit door, slipped the catches, and propped both the doors open. That should help the draught.

Still careful not to collect a dab of blood, he dragged Jeggo to the end of the courtyard and left him there. If he wanted to rush in and try to put out the fire when he came round, he was welcome to. Duffy hopped over a few fences until he came to an alley leading back out into Greek Street. There were still a few cruising taxis, looking for drunken foreign punters whom they could drive to hotels a mile away and charge them ten quid. They're a greedy bunch, cabmen, that late at night, but Duffy didn't care. When the first taxi didn't stop, he simply waved a five-pound note at the driver of the second and told him to take him to Carol's.

Eddy certainly wouldn't think that it was Duffy who had done him. Not straight away, at least. Duffy was sure Jeggo hadn't had time to see him. But Eddy might work it out by process of elimination. He might connect Duffy's security business with the fact that someone had bypassed the burglar alarm on his side room. And he might come up with a name at the same time as he realised what he had lost. What had he said that time? Great men have their libraries. Eddy had his files and tapes and films and Polaroids. Only Eddy didn't have them any more. Knowledge is Power; and without that room Big Eddy Martoff was going to be no more than just another pushy Soho villain.

Duffy didn't want to be around when Martoff realised that. He didn't like to think of Martoff running his finger down the telephone directory for Duffy's home address. So Duffy wouldn't go back to his Paddington flat, not for anything. In any case, after two burglaries there wasn't much left there that he valued. Everything was replace-able: clothes, tools, television set.

There were a few last things to do, of course, before

Duffy disappeared into another part of London. As he sat in the taxi he felt the front of his anorak. The files made him look pregnant. He'd taken two: Sullivan's and McKechnie's. In the morning, after he'd slept with them under his pillow, he'd pop round the corner and have Sullivan's Xeroxed. Five copies. He didn't worry so much about McKechnie; but Sullivan wasn't getting away.

Then he'd pack the files up, enclose the tape and transcripts Bell would have delivered to Carol's by now, and send them off to A10. He didn't know what A10 would do about McKechnie – probably pass the file on – but he knew what they'd do about Sullivan. And just to make sure that they knew what they were going to do about Sullivan, he'd send off four of the Xerox copies to crime desks in Fleet Street. The fifth he'd keep for himself. It should see Sullivan good for five years at least, depending on which judge he drew.

When Duffy got to Carol's, she was still up. The package from Bell was on the kitchen table. She hadn't seen Duffy so cheerful for months. He grinned at her, pressed his file-stuffed anorak against her and gave her a kiss. Then he looked at her oddly, shook his head an inch or two, and said, 'Sorry'. Sorry, she supposed he meant, in case you misinterpreted that. But she didn't ask. She didn't ask either what he had been doing, or why he wanted to stay the night tonight, or why she had had to put off her date. She didn't ask, because she really didn't want to know. All she said to him was,

'Duffy, I thought you might be hungry, so I've got us some bread and cheese.'

He looked up, then suddenly seemed lost in memory. He was thinking about the last few days, about the fears and the anger; he was thinking about the cubicle at the Aladdin's Lamp, and the thin copper wire wrapped threateningly around him. But all that he said to Carol by way of explanation about Martoff and Jeggo and

180

Georgiou, about Sullivan and Shaw, about McKechnie and Bell – all he said about what had happened to him in the past weeks, and what he had done, was,

'I really don't think I could face cheese, love.'

And then he gave her an enigmatic smile.

Peter Lovesey

The False Inspector Dew   71338 $2.95
"Irresistible...delightfully off-beat...wickedly clever."
—*Washington Post Book World*

Keystone   72604 $2.95

James McClure

"A distinguished crime novelist who has created in his Africaner Tromp Kramer and Bantu Sergeant Zondi two detectives who are as far from stereotypes as any in the genre."   —P.D. James, *New York Times Book Review*

The Artful Egg	72126	$3.95
The Blood of an Englishman	71019	$2.95
The Caterpillar Cop	71058	$2.95
The Gooseberry Fool	71059	$2.95
Snake	72304	$2.95
The Sunday Hangman	72992	$2.95
The Steam Pig	71021	$2.95

William McIlvanney

Laidlaw   73338 $2.95
"I have seldom been so taken by a character as I was by the angry and compassionate Glasgow detective, Laidlaw. McIlvanney is to be congratulated."   —Ross MacDonald

The Papers of Tony Veitch   73486 $2.95

Poul Ørum

Scapegoat   71335 $2.95
"Not only a very good mystery, but also a highly literate novel."

—Maj Sjöwall

Martin Page

The Man Who Stole the Mona Lisa   74098 $3.50
"Full of life and good humor....His novel is a delight."   —*New Yorker*

Julian Rathbone

"Right up there with Le Carré and company."   —*Publishers Weekly*

A Spy of the Old School	72276	$2.95
The Euro-Killers	71061	$2.95

Vassilis Vassilikos

Z   72990 $3.95
"A fascinating novel."   —*Atlantic*

Per Wahlöö

Murder on the Thirty-First Floor   70840 $2.95
"Something quite special and fascinating."   —*New York Times Book Review*

Elliot West

The Night Is a Time for Listening   74099 $3.95
"The major spy novel of the year."   —*New York Times*

Look for the Pantheon International Crime series at your local bookstore or use the coupon below to order. Prices shown are publisher's suggested retail price. Any reseller is free to charge whatever price he wishes for books listed. Prices are subject to change without notice.

Quantity	Catalog #	Price

$1.00 basic charge for postage and handling $1.00

25¢ charge per additional book

Please include applicable sales tax

Total

Send orders to: Pantheon Books, PIC 28-2, 201 East 50th St., New York, NY 10022.

Please send me the books I have listed above. I am enclosing $_____ which includes a postage and handling charge of $1.00 for the first book and 25¢ for each additional book, plus applicable sales tax. Please send check or money order in U.S. dollars only. No cash or C.O.D.'s accepted. Orders delivered in U.S. only. Please allow 4 weeks for delivery. This offer expires 7/30/87.

Name _____

Address _____

City _____ State _____ Zip _____